I Knead You Tonight

TEAGAN HUNTER

Editing by Editing by C. Marie
Proofreading by Deaton Author Services & Judy's Proofreading
Photography by Samantha Weaver Photography
Models: Courtney Marie & Joshua Lee
Makeup by: You Glow Girl by Tonya
Formatting by AB Formatting

For my real fake son Doug.
I don't know why I'm dedicating this book to you.
You're not allowed to read this.

Slice One

DREW

“You have got to be kidding me…”

Turning the key currently shoved into the ignition of my old beat-up car, I get the same result as the other four times I tried this—nothing.

“Come on, come on, come on,” I chant, trying yet again to get my car to crank.

Nada.

My eyes begin to brim with hot tears. I blink as they threaten to spill over, but I’m too late. The floodgates have opened and there’s no stopping the stream running down my cheeks.

It’s not just because my car won’t start.

It’s everything.

It’s the mounting bills, the late-night shifts, the pure and utter exhaustion that’s creeping in.

Oh, and the fact that my stupid ex-boyfriend dumped my ass when he found out I was pregnant, leaving me to take care of our baby on my own.

My lips pull into a grin as thoughts of my sweet perfect little Riker sweep through my mind.

I don't care how things pan out for me, just as long as my baby has the best life I can give him.

It's crazy, you know. They always say the moment you hold your baby in your arms, your life changes. They say everything that was important before suddenly dims in comparison, all the desires you had simply disappear, and your entire life belongs to the heartbeat in your hands.

I never believed the hype. I felt him inside of me for months and months. He had already changed my life. How was it going to be possible that I could love him even more than I already did?

Oh, I could.

I could and I do.

When I first discovered I was pregnant, I wasn't happy. I mean, who would be happy to get knocked up by some dude you've only been dating a few months, one you're basically just dating for sex anyway?

Not one single person.

I was even angrier when he left me soon after those pink lines appeared on the test. He pulled out of our future quicker than he ever pulled out of me.

Hence where I'm at in life.

Exhausted. Broke. Single mom to a healthy, beautiful three-month-old.

And I wouldn't change a single moment of any of it.

I push my shoulders back and give myself a shake, wiping the drying tears from my cheeks and not letting yet another setback get me down.

Besides, I don't have time for that. I need to get home to relieve my sitter, and no one is going to make that happen except me.

So, the city bus it is. Again. *Ugh.*

You've got this, Drew. It's fine. You're fine. Things will be just fucking fine.

They have to be.

For Riker.

I grip the door handle and reach for my bag where I stashed it in the passenger seat. I grab my phone charger and make sure to shove it inside the black pit I call a purse so I can charge my phone tonight.

You know, the one that's at approximately fifteen percent.

"Because why wouldn't it be dead," I mutter, shoving the car door open.

"MY DICK!"

A scream rips from my lips and I yank the door closed again, watching as a dark figure crumples to the ground right outside my car.

I jam down the lock button, the click deafening inside the vehicle. My heart hammers in my chest, my heavy breaths fogging up the chilled glass in an instant.

The stranger lies on the ground and I can barely make out the curses slipping from his lips.

"Son of a bitch." A loud, manly groan rumbles from his curled form. "This is what I get for being a fucking gentleman? Fuck this shit. Dammit, my fucking dick is on fire."

I stifle the giggle that's threatening to bubble out of me, not wanting to bring attention to myself. Maybe if I feign invisibility, he'll go away.

A weighty hand lands on the handle as the man peels himself up off the ground.

I can hear his breathing through the window.

It's harsh. Thick.

Or is that me?

"Fucking fuck," he curses.

A cap-covered head pops up over the edge of the car door, his head hanging there for a moment, another groan escaping his mouth before a familiar pair of bright blue eyes meets my scared, drab brown ones.

My brows pinch together, and I'm no longer trying to hold back a laugh.

No. Now I'm *furious.*

I thrust the door open and my would-be attacker stumbles backward, jumping a few feet and catching himself before he goes down again.

"Hey! Watch the dick! You already nailed me once tonight."

I climb out of my broken-down clunker and stomp toward him, shoving at his hard chest.

"Oh, you wish I'd nail you, Winston Daniels!"

My best friend's twin brother and my mortal enemy grins at me with his signature *Come and get it* smirk.

I want to reach out and smack it off his face.

In general, I like my waitressing job at Slice. Not only is the pizzeria a tourist destination, making the tips nice, the people I work with make dealing with the general public feel like a breeze.

You know, minus Winston.

To put it simply, Winston Daniels is the most annoying man on the planet—and my ex-boyfriend left me when I was pregnant, so that's saying something.

He's arrogant. Lazy. Has no care in the world for anyone but himself.

And I despise him.

"Quit smiling, you ass!"

I push him again, and this time he laughs.

"Stop it!"

Another laugh. "Nah."

"Winston!"

His booming laugh echoes throughout the empty parking lot and I roll my eyes, storming off.

A strong hand curls around my wrist and I'm spun in place until I hit a brick wall.

Or perhaps that's Winston's chest.

Right now, they feel the same.

"What?" I seethe.

He drops his eyes to where my hands are planted on his chest, raising a brow at the contact.

I try to take a step back, but he won't let me move.

"Where do you think you're going?"

"Home. Obviously."

"Your car won't start—*again*, I might add."

"No shit, Sherlock." I try to wiggle out of his grasp, but he still won't relent. I huff. "Let me go. I have a bus to catch."

"No."

My brows shoot into my hairline at the flippancy in his tone. "Excuse me?"

"You heard me. You're not riding the fucking bus home."

"Then what am I supposed to do? Walk?"

"No."

"Right. Let me just grab my wrench from my purse, pop the hood, and get this thing fixed myself."

"Is it just me or are you extra pissy tonight?"

I don't know if it's the facetious smirk on his face or the way he says it, but I break.

Completely and wholly.

The tears spring back into my eyes and blood rushes to my face as I shove and shove at Winston's chest.

"What the—" He stumbles, brows slashed together, lips drawn into a thin line.

"Fuck you, Daniels! Fuck you and your stupid bullshit. You don't even know what real life is. You live in some damn fantasy world where you think life is nothing but flowers and rainbows. You wouldn't know real life if it bit you in the ass."

"I wouldn't?"

"No!" I shout. "You don't know what it's like to struggle, to beg the electric company to not turn your heat off, to live off ramen so you can make sure your baby has food and diapers. You don't know shit about shit, Winston."

"I know you're not taking the fucking bus."

I growl at his arrogance, swiping at the hot tears. "You're not my boss. You're not anything to me but a turd on the bottom of my shoe. You're the—"

"Did you just call me a turd?"

"Yes! Because you are one! You're—"

"At least you didn't call me a penis wrinkle like Wren's taken to doing. That one is just…" He shakes his head like none of this is affecting him, like he thinks it's some comedy sketch when in reality I am getting precariously close to the end of my rope. "It's odd."

"Are you fucking kidding me right now?"

"No. She really calls me a penis wrinkle. How have you not heard her say it? You two are attached at the hip so I find this hard to believe."

He's not wrong about his sister and me, but that's completely beside the point right now.

"You're just going to stand there talking about penis wrinkles while I'm having a meltdown?"

"What else am I supposed to do?"

"Anything other than that! Literally anything but talk about penis wrinkles."

He lifts a shoulder. "I don't have anything else to say."

"Nothing? Not a damn thing?"

"No."

The way he stares at me, like he doesn't give a crap about any of the things plaguing my life…it hurts.

I can't choke back the sob that bubbles up in my throat.

Thick arms wrap around me, stopping my descent before my knees hit the dirty ground, and I'm engulfed in warmth as my cries fill the night.

I don't know how long we stand here, but it's long enough for a wet spot to form on Winston's shirt.

Everything I've bottled up for months breaks free. All the late nights, the financial stress, the relationship woes…all of it. I cry it all out, pushing the emotion from my body like I never have before because I need this moment. I need this relief.

I don't care that I'm breaking down in front of my mortal enemy.

This isn't about him. This moment is about me.

Winston shifts, his arms flexing around me, and I don't miss how small I feel inside his embrace.

Has he always been this big compared to me? Has he always been this chiseled? Is he always this warm?

"Knock it off."

His gruff voice interrupts any inkling of nice thoughts I have regarding him.

I can't even muster the strength to glare up at him, but his words make me cry harder.

"I said fucking stop. Quit crying, Drew."

"F-Fuck you," I stutter.

"No thanks." He squeezes me, like he can somehow magically

tighten his grip and get me to stop. "I'm serious—stop crying."

"You can't just command someone to not cry. That's not how it works."

"I fucking wish it did. I hate this shit."

I push away from him. "Well, if you think I like crying in front of you, you're wrong." I swipe at the tears and snot covering my face. "If I gave a shit what you thought about me, this would be embarrassing as hell." I give him a saccharine grin. "But I hate you, so I don't give a fuck."

He snorts out a laugh, pulling the cigarette tucked behind his ear free and lighting it up, taking a big hit of nicotine before blowing the cloud of smoke my way. "Right. You hate me."

I wave away the stench and scowl at him. "So much more than you think."

He doesn't say anything to that, just grins around his cancer stick and stares at me with those annoyingly beautiful baby blues.

The thing I hate most about Winston is that I don't hate the way he looks.

I don't hate it at all.

Speaking from my most basic human instincts, Winston Daniels is fuckable.

But I'll be the last person to ever fuck him.

He's traditionally attractive with a strong, square jaw that's perpetually lined with stubble, light brown hair that curls in just the right way when grown out, and don't even get me started on his eyes.

The brightest blue I've ever seen.

Flawless in their beauty yet filled with secrets.

I hate them almost as much as I hate him because they make me want to know everything he's hiding.

The cloud of smoke he's created swirls around him, and right now he's the picturesque version of a bad boy. Dark boots, tight jeans, a simple black tee, and a flannel shirt tied around his waist. The very muscles I just had my hands on strain with every movement he makes. Even if I hadn't felt them for myself, it's clear Winston spends a lot of time working out. I mean, what else is he supposed to do with all his free time since he hardly shows up to work at his dad's pizzeria and has no other discernable extracurricular activities besides chasing beach bunnies?

"Like what you see?"

I roll my eyes. "Please. You wish."

He grins again, and I ignore the pinch I feel between my legs.

Fucking traitorous body.

I brush the stray hairs back from my face and pull my jacket tighter around me, ready to take my leave because I can't stand to spend one more minute in his presence. I need to get home.

"You better not say a word to anyone about this," I warn as I brush past him.

His hand wraps around my wrist yet again, stopping me in my tracks.

"Let me go, Winston. I really need to get home, and the bus will be here in less than ten minutes. Some of us have responsibilities, you know."

He ignores me, taking one last puff of his cigarette before tossing the butt to the side.

"What'd I tell you?"

I scrunch my nose, not sure what he's getting at. "That you have penis wrinkles?"

"No. That you're not riding the bus."

I groan and try to pull free again.

He doesn't concede. If anything, his grip tightens more, and I wonder briefly if I'll have bruises tomorrow morning.

"Just let me the fuck go!"

"NO!"

I stumble, blinking up as his six-two frame towers over me. It's the first time he's shown any real emotion tonight, and I don't know how to process it.

"I said no." He's speaking quietly now, but his voice is still firm.

"Then what the hell am I supposed to do? I was just kidding about the wrench."

He tugs on my arm and I have to fight to keep my balance as he begins dragging me in the opposite direction of the bus stop.

My heart stutters as he pulls me farther into the dark parking lot, away from the building—away from anything, in fact.

"W-Winston? Where are we going?"

"You're coming home with me."

Slice Two

WINSTON

This last strand of bud had to have been laced with something that's fried my brain cells permanently.

It's the only explanation I can come up with as to why I would tell Drew Woods she's coming home with me.

Well, Drew *and* her baby.

I fucking hate babies.

And I hate Drew.

Yeah. That bud is really goddamn strong.

She's been quiet the entire ride. Hasn't spoken a peep since I finally convinced her to get in my station wagon and let me give her a ride.

I pull my old beater—the same one that saved my life—into Drew's apartment complex and cut the engine.

She's out of the vehicle faster than I ever thought possible.

No *Thanks for the ride.* Not even a *Fuck you.*

Just gone.

I dive out of the car, following close behind her.

"Seriously?" she shoots over her shoulder, voice full of venom—which is funny considering I just drove completely out of my way for her. "Do you have to follow me inside?"

"Yes."

"Why?"

"I think we both know I don't trust you to come back out here, and I was very serious about you coming home with me."

She whirls around and I nearly run into her, catching myself at the last second because the last thing I want to do is feel Drew in my arms again.

Holding her in the parking lot was enough physical contact for one night. It was all I could possibly handle.

I might hate Drew, but my dick wasn't getting that message earlier.

Sure, Drew's cute. She always has been.

But something changed about her when she got pregnant.

It's like she stopped pretending to be someone else and finally accepted herself, and not just because she let her dark hair grow out and had my sister Wren strip it back down to its natural blonde.

It's more than her appearance.

It's her.

She's still mouthy as ever, but she's much more confident than she's ever been—and that's saying something because Drew is the most confident chick I've ever met.

"In what world does me going home with you make *any* sense? The animosity between us is palpable, Winston, not to mention I have a *baby*. I can't bring Riker to your house and just set up camp. That's not how things work."

"In what world can't you do that? Put some diapers in a bag and get your ass in the car. It's not as difficult as you're trying to make it."

"Fine. How about I don't *want* to go home with you? Are you understanding what I'm saying now?"

I laugh. "You think I want you in my home? Think I'm so fucking eager to have baby crap strewn all over the place and I'm just *dying* to be woken up in the middle of the night by a curdling scream? Think again."

"Then why are you so insistent on me coming with you?" Her angry voice echoes around the lot and I swear I hear someone yell out their window in the distance. Her chest heaves up and down as she works to catch her breath, eyes wide, surprised at her own outburst.

"Because despite how much you like to paint me as one, I'm not a monster, Drew. I can't leave you at your apartment without a vehicle when you have a three-month-old baby. What if something happens to him? To you? What if Riker gets sick? What are you going to do, Drew? Wait on the bus schedule to post and hope and pray it gets here on time? Fuck that. I'm not willing to gamble your life or your baby's like that."

Her mouth hangs open. Closes. Opens.

Slowly, her full lips curve into a cloying smile, like I just hung the fucking moon or some shit.

"What?" I bite out when she doesn't say anything, just continues to stare at me.

"You care."

"Excuse me?"

"You care. About me. About Riker."

"I don't even know your gremlin."

"No, but you care about me, and Riker is a part of me so you care about him too."

I groan. "Whatever story you need to weave to get you both back into my car, weave it. Let's just get this show on the road. I have an early morning tomorrow."

"You? An early morning? Doing what—jacking your dick?"

"No. I'll be doing that tonight. Mornings are reserved for something a little less naughty but just as fun." I nod toward the apartment complex. "Get moving. We're on a schedule."

With a huff, she turns on her heel, and I follow closely behind her.

She takes the stairs slowly, like she's stalling for time, and it's physically hurting me to walk this slowly.

"What's your damage now?"

She peeks back at me, her bottom lip stuck firmly between her teeth. "It's just...well, don't judge me by my apartment, okay? I'm doing the best I can."

"I would never judge you, Drew."

And it's true. I wouldn't.

Judging isn't my style, and I know how hard she's been working to make ends meet. I see it every day. She comes in with eyes puffy from lack of sleep. Her hair sometimes looks like it hasn't been combed in days. She pulls and twists at her neck, trying to get the knots to loosen up for just a few minutes of relief.

I see it all.

It's the reason I've been picking up so much slack around Slice.

I'll be the first to admit I'm known for being unreliable when it comes to working in my dad's pizzeria, but that's because some days the pain is just too much to bear and I have to smoke myself numb to make it through.

Lately, though, I've been cutting back on the smoking and trying to fight through the pain.

For Drew.

The day she came in with tears streaking down her face, her lips bleeding from her biting at them through an anxiety attack…I knew.

I had to step up.

The only blessing in her situation is that she's easily distracted. I've been using it to my advantage for weeks now, getting her riled up about something at work so she doesn't notice me slipping my tips into her apron.

Either she never counts her money during her shift, or she's just walking around thinking she's an extraordinary waitress.

Not that what I slip her is a lot, because *I'm* a horrible waiter, but it's something, and something goes a long way when you have a baby and no one else to help.

Sometimes I feel guilty about that.

Drew stops at a door, knocking twice before shooting me another cautious glance.

I ignore her, eyes locked on the door, eager to see who is on the other side.

We can hear movement and it's pulled open just a crack, a face looking back out at us.

Her face is slim, eyes big, and cheeks rosy. She's young, that's for sure. Still a teenager if I'm not mistaken.

The young girl must recognize Drew because she pulls the door open farther, but she hesitates to open it wider when she sees me standing behind her. Her brows lift in a silent question.

"He's with me," Drew answers.

The girl nods, pulling the door open completely. Low music drifts from within, and I note that it's dated for her age.

"I am *so* sorry I'm late, Doris. My car broke down."

"Again?" the girl says, sounding just as exasperated as Drew.

"I know." Drew holds her hand up. "I know. Don't even get me started. It's been a long week, but never mind all that and my dramas. How's my sweet boy doing?"

Doris smiles widely. "He's wonderful. He just fell asleep about an hour ago."

"Aw, I hate to have to wake him."

"I'm sure he's looking forward to seeing his mama."

"I—" Drew looks back at me, like she forgot I was there for a minute, all her attention having shifted to her son. "Here." She hands her lanyard to me. "It's apartment 4B. The key with the flowers on it will open the door. I'll meet you up there in a few minutes."

I grab the keys from Drew's outstretched hand, figuring the girl who can't be a day over sixteen—whose name is dated right along with her musical taste—looks harmless enough.

Racing up the steps two at a time, I slide the lock into the door and push it open, unsure what I'm going to see on the other side.

My throat begins to close as soon as I step into the room.

Because that's all it is—a room.

Drew's been living in this tiny-ass apartment—*with her baby*—while I've been living it up in a fucking two-bedroom house.

I'm a jackass.

Not only is the apartment—or more accurately, the bedroom—small, it's just as cold in here as it is outside.

I close the door.

Nope, still too cold.

Especially for a baby.

Drew mentioned she was behind on her bills, but I didn't realize she was *this* behind on them.

The guilt seeps in just a bit more.

Glancing around the room, I begin picking it apart.

The paint is peeling, and there's a bucket in the corner clearly placed there to collect the water dripping from the ceiling. Cabinet doors are missing. There's a musty smell Drew's tried to cover with the candles littered about.

It's not the worst thing I've seen, but it's not ideal, especially with the lack of heating.

I step farther into the room, looking over the very personal items strewn about.

It's mostly kid toys—rattles and other noisy shit—but there are a few things of hers lying about too.

A romance novel is splayed across the arm of the couch, holding her spot for whenever she gets another free moment to read, something I know she used to love doing.

A grocery list and a pen with a mercilessly chewed-on cap sit on the coffee table next to an abandoned blue bracelet and a pair of earrings.

A single photo of Drew and Riker in the hospital sits in the center of the small entertainment center next to an old, outdated laptop.

Other than that, the place is sparse.

No decorations. No other photos. Nothing.

She doesn't even have a bed for crying out loud. She's been sleeping on the couch.

It's like she doesn't plan to be here long enough to settle in.

The door behind me rattles as Drew tries to push it open and I pull on the knob, knowing her hands are going to be full of Riker and his things.

"Thanks," she mutters, barreling through the door. "I'll just grab some of his stuff real quick and we can get going. It's way past his bedtime."

"Just tell me what he needs, and I can grab it."

"It'll be much faster if I do it. You have no idea what's what."

I roll my eyes. "I'm not incompetent, Drew. I can deduce what a baby does and doesn't need."

"Fine." She turns her lips down at the corners, hating to accept the help but knowing it'll be better in the end so she doesn't risk waking up the baby.

I roam around the room, stuffing some diapers, formula canisters, bottles, wipes, plenty of clothes, blankets, and a few toys into the two different diaper bags I find as Drew coos and sings to a sleeping Riker.

"Shit, Winston, how long do you think we're staying with you?"

"As long as you need to," I answer simply.

I pull open the only two drawers on the small, raggedy dresser that must belong to her and she squeaks from behind me.

"Wait! Those are my drawers."

"Yes," I say, holding up a pair of baby blue lacy underwear. "I assumed this isn't something Riker would wear."

"Put my panties down," she urges through clenched teeth.

"Relax. It's not like I'm going to stand here sniffing all your underwear in front of you." I tuck the lacy garment into my front pocket. "I'll save that for later."

"I hate you." She shoots a fiery stare my way, wanting so desperately to charge at me and wrestle the panties from my pocket but knowing there's nothing she can do about it right now.

I grab a handful of underwear and socks, shoving them into another bag I found. I grab some tees and pants, enough to get her by.

"If you need something else, we can stop by later, or just hit up the store."

She snorts. "Right, like I have spare cash to spend on new clothes."

I tighten my jaw at the comment, trying not to dwell on it or her situation for too long.

"You ready?" I ask, my arms loaded down with bags for them

both, enough stuff to last a week.

"To stay with you? Never, but what choice do I have?" She sighs. "Let me get him into his car seat and get this hell over with."

"No. Absolutely not."

Drew stands before me, hands on her hips, eyes puffy with tiredness.

She's exhausted, beyond so. Which is why I offered her my bed.

Well, that and she can't sleep on the couch with Riker and I have nowhere else to put him. My bad because I clearly didn't think this whole *You're coming home with me* thing through.

"Well, tough fucking tits. It's happening."

"You can't seriously expect me to sleep in your bed and take over your room while you sleep on that dilapidated couch, Winston. I hate you, but damn—I gotta draw the line somewhere."

"I'm offering it to you. I'm choosing this. Just accept it and quit bitching about the handout."

Drew's jaw tightens. I don't know if it's the truth behind my words that gets her angry or the word choice.

Either way, she knows I'm right.

I'm letting her stay here free of charge when it's painfully clear she desperately needs the help but is too fucking stubborn to ask for it.

Riker coos and we both glance his way, silencing any argument Drew might have made.

She knows she needs to do this for him.

I'm not a baby person at all, but even I can admit the little bundle of jelly rolls is adorable as hell. He's still buckled into his car seat nice and tight, having slept the entire way over here, not making a single peep when she carried him inside. I'm certain that means he's out for the night.

Thank fuck, because I could really use the sleep.

"At least let me repay you for all of this."

"With all that money you don't have?" I scoff. "You couldn't even keep your fucking heat on, Drew. I don't see how you're going to pay me for letting you stay here."

Her eyes flash with anger again, but she brushes off my insult. "It was on when I left for work this morning. I wouldn't have stayed there with my son if I didn't have heat. I'd never put him through that. But that's not what we're talking about right now. I can repay you for letting us stay here in other ways."

"Please tell me you mean sexual favors." I smirk. "I would love to fill that sassy mouth of yours with my cock."

I say it to fuck with her, because lord knows I don't mean it.

Heat steals up her cheeks and her breaths become uneven, and I can't tell if it's because she loves the idea or hates it.

She screws her face up. "You're disgusting."

But there's no bite behind her words.

"That wasn't a no."

"I am *not* giving you sexual favors. I meant like help around the house. Doing dishes, cooking…those sorts of things."

"Those don't sound nearly as satisfying as blow jobs."

"Get out, Winston," she huffs.

Laughing, I pull the door mostly shut behind me, leaving her there to stew.

After stopping at the hall closet to grab a fresh set of sheets, I make my way to the living room.

I pluck the fitted sheet from the pile, slipping it around the couch cushions as best I can.

"Is it just me or do you have a thing for taking in strays?" I hear the recliner squeak as my roommate, Sully, takes a seat. "I could have given her my room, you know."

I peer back at him. "No way, man. I'm the one who offered to let her stay here. This was my bad decision."

He snorts in the way only he can.

The way that says *There's more to your story, but I'll let it slide for now.*

"You know the rules, Sully—if there's something you want to say, just fucking say it. Don't do that hippie mind-reading bullshit with me."

"I just think it's funny you're calling this a bad decision."

"Why's that?"

"Because something inevitable can't be a bad decision. Not when it was meant to be all along."

"What the fuck does that even mean?"

"You know. Deep down, you know."

I groan, pinching the bridge of my nose between my fingers. "I'm convinced you're the reason I smoke so much sometimes. It's so I can get your bullshit out of my head."

"I don't doubt that," he agrees.

I plop down onto the sofa, and though the linens are fresh, they do nothing to hide how uncomfortable this damn thing is. "How the hell did I let Foster sleep on this for so long?"

"Because you're a good friend."

"You're only saying that because I let you stay here for free."

"True." Sully laughs, pushing up from the chair and grabbing his surfboard that's resting against the wall. "I'm heading out."

I want to tell him he's an idiot for surfing at night, that anything could happen out there in the dark, but I know he'll just argue that anything could happen in the daylight too.

"Enjoy your therapy," I mutter.

The back door slides shut, and I pull out my phone, setting myself a reminder to make an appointment at the local auto shop first thing tomorrow morning. I know Harvey Schwartz will fit me in, especially considering how much money I've spent there keeping my station wagon alive and chugging.

It's the same old clunker my mom used to drive us around in, and I couldn't let it go.

I click the lamp off and lie back on the couch, arms crossed under my head, trying to get my brain to settle down, something it never wants to do at night.

Not since the accident.

Nearly three years ago now, I was clipped coming home from a party in college.

The road was winding, dark, dangerous…wet from hours of rain.

I was lucky, limping away with only a broken collarbone, a fractured leg, and a whole slew of chiropractor appointments from messed-up discs in my back and neck.

The other driver walked away with minimal damage physically, but not financially.

When her toxicology report came back, we found out she was drunk off her ass…something my lawyer didn't let slide by without a big stink, especially considering she was the mayor's daughter.

I took the insanely large settlement they offered and bought this house in cash, setting me up for a long time to come. Then I went about my life like I didn't see the accident on replay every time I closed my eyes.

The joke was on me though.

I blew off too many doctors, too much physical therapy, and now I've left my body beyond repair.

The light sound of music drifts from my bedroom and I can't

quite make out what it is. Probably a kiddie lullaby or some shit.

I turn to my side, hiding my face from the light coming through around the door. The second I turn, I feel it.

The aching that won't go away.

The one that hurts so bad I can't sleep at night…unless I smoke until I can't see straight.

I'm aware of the fact that this constant pain is partly my own doing.

After my accident, everyone looked at me like I was this broken, fragile thing. I couldn't handle it. Every day I was still strapped into that sling or being whisked off to physical therapy, it was another day they were staring at me like I was shattered. I couldn't fucking stand it. The moment I declared I was healed, they all started treating me differently.

I learned pretty fast I was free from the looks, but not from the pain.

It didn't matter though. I found my cure.

It didn't matter how many ibuprofens I downed; they didn't touch the throbbing…or the storm that seemed to constantly be brewing inside me. The only thing that chased it all away was weed.

If I'm not high, I'm just…done. Empty. The only thing I feel anymore is pain, and the only thing that makes me not feel the pain is pot.

I smoke so I can feel alive again and not like I'm going to explode if I move the wrong way.

Sure, it pisses me off that the people I love most only see me as this stoner who's always blowing everyone off, but I can't give it up.

It's the only thing that works.

With an irritated growl, I push myself up off the couch, trying to ignore the stabbing pain that's traveling through my body. I grab my box and my lighter, heading outside so I can smoke in peace.

Stepping onto the patio, I pop open my metal tin and pull out a joint. I slide the sweet relief between my lips and flick the lighter, watching the end glow red as I inhale.

I puff a few times, getting the joint glowing like I like. When it's lit enough, I close my eyes, finally taking a long toke and holding it in my lungs as long as possible.

Just like that, the pain isn't so bad. My mind isn't racing in circles.

When I open my eyes again, Drew's stepping through my cloud of smoke.

She stops a foot away from me, arms crossed over her chest, tits pushed up. "I'm sorry if the music was too loud. I can turn it down."

I ignore her and take another long hit, chasing the quiet I crave.

"Look, if we're an inconvenience, we can leave. We've been surviving just fine without you. We'll make do."

"Not everything is about you, Drew."

"Well, excuse me for assuming so, especially since you're out here in this freezing weather."

"It's not even cold."

"It's fifty, and you live on the beach. It's *freezing*."

"Or you're just a pussy."

"Ugh." She groans. "Can't you just not be an ass for like five minutes?"

"Can't you just leave me alone for five minutes? I'm giving you and your kid a place to stay. All I want to do is smoke in peace."

"Whatever." She turns toward the door I left open. "Look, not that I want to tell you what to do in your own house or anything, but I'd really appreciate if you didn't do that around Riker."

I hold the joint up. "I'm out here, aren't I?"

She glowers and stalks back inside, making a scene out of closing the back door.

I lean against the railing, not letting her touch these fleeting moments of tranquility.

The overhead light in my bedroom is turned off, only the lamp illuminating the space.

From where I'm standing, I can see into the room through the slit in the curtains.

I can see Drew.

See her unbutton the jeans she's wearing. See her stomach peek out of the stretch between her underwear and her shirt.

She pulls it over her head, moving out of my line of sight, but not before I spot the strap of a light blue bra.

Just like the light blue of the underwear I stole.

The pair still resting in my pocket.

I slide my hand inside my jeans, feeling the material slip through my fingers.

I was just screwing with her earlier when I took them. I would never sniff her underwear like some fucking pervert.

But I'm also in no hurry to give the sliver of fabric back to her.

I don't know why. Just like I don't know why she felt so good in my arms earlier.

I don't know why I want to feel her in them again.

Giving myself a shake, I turn my back to the window and take another drag off the joint between my fingers.

Damn, this is some good weed.

Slice Three

DREW

What the…

I glance around the unfamiliar room, forgetting for a moment I had a lapse in sanity last night and agreed to let Winston have me and Riker stay with him while my car is getting fixed.

"Shit…my car. I need to schedule something."

"I already did."

"JESUS FUCK!" I yelp, leaping out of the bed.

Thankfully my mommy instincts are so ingrained in me now that I leap *away* from my sleeping baby.

"What the hell are you doing in here, Winston? And why are you *naked?*"

"Well, for starters, I'm not naked. I'm clearly wearing a towel. And I'm in here because this is *my* bedroom, in case you forgot, which means this"—he points to the adjacent bathroom—"is my bathroom."

Well shit. He's got me there.

"Do you have to shower while I'm sleeping?"

"Considering it's after nine in the morning and I've been up since before the sunrise, yes."

"It's after nine?" My mouth drops open, my fingers reaching for my cell phone on the bedside table, checking to see if he's just screwing with me or not.

He's not.

"Holy shit." I sit back on the bed, staring down at my still-sleeping angel. "I don't remember the last time I slept this late. I'm usually woken up by Riker wanting food or screaming from my neighbors or something else obnoxious happening in the complex."

Winston shrugs. "You're welcome."

"For?"

"Giving you a quiet place to sleep."

"Thanks," I mumble, annoyed I had to resort to sleeping over at Winston Daniels' house to get a good night's sleep.

I push up out of the bed, rummaging around in our bags to get our things ready for the day.

"He should probably wake up though. He started fussing before I got in the shower. Turns out the kid loves Slayer."

I raise my brows. "You played him Slayer?"

"I sang it to him until he calmed down."

"You sang Slayer to my baby?"

"Yes?" He says it as a question, pulling open the dresser drawer I'm standing next to. I try not to let my eyes trail down his naked chest, try not to watch the muscles in his body jump. "Is that not okay?"

"No, no, it's fine. I just kind of wish I had it on video or something…for blackmail later. Proof that you *do* have a heart."

"Oh, was the generosity of letting you stay here not enough?"

I sigh. "Are you going to do that the entire time we're here? Throw my inability to pay my bills in my face? If so, you can shove your generosity straight up your ass."

He turns toward me, and I realize then just how close we are, his chest nearly brushing against mine.

The way his body felt against mine last night lingers in my mind, and I want to step closer and farther away all at once.

But I stand my ground, not wanting to appear weak.

"I'm sorry."

His words send a shockwave through me.

"Excuse me?"

He narrows his eyes. "You heard me, and I won't repeat it. But you're right. I shouldn't be throwing it in your face. I won't say anything again."

He turns back to the dresser, and I miss his heat the moment he does.

"You said you wanted to repay me, right?"

"Anything. Name it." I hold my hand up. "Wait—anything *not* sexual."

His lips pull up at the corners. "Go shopping with me."

"I already told you I don't have any money."

"It's not for you, it's for me. I need a new couch. That one out there is horrible."

I wince but refuse to apologize.

Us staying here was his idea, not mine.

"I'd like to get a sectional or something bigger, get rid of that old recliner out there too. You game?"

"You game with toting around a three-month-old baby all day?"

"Wait, you're telling me Riker *can't* stay home and watch himself yet? What a little shitbag." He rolls his eyes. "Yes, I'm obviously fine with him coming along."

"Okay then. We're in."

"We can stop at Slice for breakfast if you want."

"Like…us together…in public…at our place of employment?"

"I don't love the idea of it either, but a free breakfast is a free breakfast, right?"

It's a fair point. I don't need to be wasting money eating out right now.

"Fine. We can go to Slice. We're sitting in different booths though."

He gives me a *Don't be dramatic* look, grabs whatever it was he was searching for, and heads toward the bathroom but doesn't shut the door, at least not all the way.

There's a crack, just big enough for me to see through.

He drops his towel, and my heart goes right along with it.

I can see everything.

His muscled back.

His perfectly taut ass.

His cock when he turns toward the mirror.

My eyes trail back up his body, only to find him staring at me in the mirror, smirking.

Gulping, I don't avert my gaze, trying to act like I don't give a shit that Winston Daniels just caught me looking at his dick. His *big* dick, I might add.

I care.

I really care.

The last thing I want is for him to think I like him or something, especially when that's not even kind of true. It's just my stupid fucking hormones making me stare at his giant dong like I haven't ever seen a penis before.

It has to be.

Because it surely has nothing to do with the fact that it's him.

Without breaking eye contact, he reaches for the boxer briefs he has sitting on the counter, bending slightly to pull them on.

When he's fully covered, I look away, and he finally shuts the door the rest of the way, laughing as he does so.

Asshole.

I slide Riker's car seat into an empty booth at Slice, trying to avoid the curious stares from my coworkers.

We didn't think this one through, us showing up together with my baby *and* my car still sitting in the parking lot at open. It looks like we spent the night together, and I guess technically we did, but not in the way I'm certain they're assuming.

They're all too pussy to come out and ask me, though.

"Did you two fuck last night?"

Well, except my best friend Wren. She doesn't give any shits.

"Trade me spots," she bosses at me. "I want to sit next to my son."

I'm not about to argue with her, especially since all *her son* did the entire ride here was cry and scream.

She can sit next to him all she wants. I need a break.

Slipping from the booth, I realize too late the only place I can go is next to Winston…who I haven't spoken to since this morning.

The ride here was short by mileage standards, but it felt hours long in the game of who can stay quiet the longest.

Riker definitely lost.

Winston grins up at me—that same obnoxious grin he's been giving me since he caught me looking at him—as he scoots over…the minimum distance that can be considered reasonable.

Our arms rub together when I sit down and the hair on mine stands at attention. The denim of his jeans rubs against my black leggings and I can feel the heat radiating off him.

Or maybe that's just me.

I've been burning up since we locked eyes in the bathroom and Winston caught me staring at his cock.

The throb I felt between my legs earlier returns, and as if he knows I'm thinking about this morning, Winston spreads his thighs wider, his leg now plastered against mine.

I pull at the collar of my shirt.

I see Winston smirk out of the corner of my eye.

Dick.

"Well, did you?" Wren asks, not looking at either of us, her attention focused on my baby.

I groan. "Don't be gross. You know we didn't."

"That's not what it looks like."

"I know that, but we didn't."

"Her car broke down again," Winston explains. "Did you know your best friend had no heat in her apartment when I went over there last night?"

Wren turns her stare to me. It's calm. Too calm.

She's pissed.

"Please tell me my idiot twin brother is just spouting off bullshit again and that's not true."

I don't say anything.

"Drew Amanda Woods!"

"Your middle name is Amanda too?" Winston pipes in.

"No. Your sister is just insane and uses her middle name for mine because I refuse to tell her mine."

"That embarrassing, huh?"

"I cannot fucking believe you, Drew!" Wren seethes, ignoring the side conversation Winston and I are having. "You've been living there without heat?"

"No. The electric company is a bag of dicks. They shut it off on me yesterday when I was at work *after* I arranged to pay the bill late. But, whatever. It's not *that* cold outside, and they would have turned it back on for me. We would have been okay for a night or two with some extra blankets."

"It's cold for a baby!"

"He would have been fine. I'd have made sure," I argue. "And I have space heaters I could have used. We'd have made it work until I got them to turn it back on."

"Dude. No." Wren frowns. "What if it drops ten degrees overnight? What then? The space heater isn't going to touch that. You need help, with *anything*"—she stresses the word and I know she means money—"call me."

"I get it, I'm a fuckup."

"No, you're just stubborn as hell. Why didn't you say anything to any of us? We wouldn't have judged."

"I'm paying the bill next week. It was only temporary."

"Temporary," Wren repeats, shaking her head. "And staying with anyone else would have been only temporary too."

"You know I don't like asking for handouts," I mutter, embarrassed.

"Well, you better get fucking used to it!" Her voice rises two octaves. "You're not asking for you anymore—you're asking for Riker. Stop being stubborn for him."

She's right. I know she's right.

Which is why I accepted Winston's offer to let us stay with him last night. He's the last person on the face of the planet I'd want to stay with, but I'm doing it.

For Riker.

"I accepted Winston's help," I tell her.

Wren looks to Winston and I swear they have one of their weird twin moments or something, because Wren's lips slowly tilt into a grin and she calms down.

"Look, I'm sorry, Drew. I just love you and Riker so much, and I don't want you two to go without anything, especially not the basics like heat."

"We're okay, Wren. I had everything handled. If it was that bad, I would have said something."

"Just don't wait at all next time, okay? I'm here. Always."

"I won't," I promise her.

"What are you doing about her car?" she asks Winston.

"Harvey Schwartz is picking it up this morning. He's gonna try to fit it in whenever he can around his other work. I told him no rush on it."

"No rush?" I interject. "There is definitely a rush. I can't go without a car for an indefinite amount of time."

"Yes, you can."

I point to my son, who is now cradled in Wren's arms. "No, I can't."

Winston slumps into the booth, scrubbing a hand over his face. "You're staying with me as long as it takes. A week, a month, a year—I don't care. Just shut the fuck up and accept it already."

I gape at him because he can't be serious.

"And yes, before you ask, I'm dead serious. Now, if you don't mind, I need to piss and you're in my way."

I stare at him, genuinely confused about how he can sound so sincere and so irritated at the same time.

"Move," he barks.

I jump at the sudden sound and scramble out of the booth, glaring at him as he brushes by me with a grunt.

"What is his deal?"

"Maybe it's your stubbornness that's irritating him," Wren offers. "Or perhaps he's realizing he's going to have to somehow survive with your fine piece of ass sleeping in the other room for god knows how long. Can you say sexually frustrated?"

She smirks up at me. If she weren't holding my baby, I'd slap the smirk right off her face for even suggesting that Winston could possibly be attracted to me and she knows it.

She's using Riker as her shield.

"Remind me again why I'm friends with you?"

"My charming personality."

"Nah, it's definitely her ass."

Foster, Wren's fiancé, appears next to me.

"You're right. I am insanely attracted to my best friend's ass. Good call, Foster."

"I knew it." He grins, and I swear it makes him look ten times hotter when he does. It's not that I'm into my friend's guy, but it's clear to anyone with eyes that Foster Marlett is hot. "What's up with you and my best friend showing up here together this morning? Did you two fuck?"

I lied. Foster isn't hot at all.

"That's what I said!" Wren exclaims. "But they didn't. Her car broke down and then Winston discovered she doesn't have heat, so she's staying with him."

"You don't have heat? What the shit? Why didn't you call us?"

I groan. "I am not going over this again."

"I said the same thing," Wren whispers, putting Riker back into his car seat. "I got my head bit off."

"You're no longer holding my baby. I'd watch it, Wren."

Poking her tongue out at me, she pulls herself out of the booth. "I'm not scared. Besides, you'd never hurt me. Then who would do your hair for you when you decide you want a change again?"

"It's still so weird seeing you with lighter hair," Foster remarks. "But I like it. It feels more…*you.*"

"That's because it is me," I say, taking Wren's spot, glad she's leaving so I don't have to sit next to Winston when he comes back. "Where are you two headed off to this morning?"

"The courthouse. We're getting hitched."

"Bullshit you are!"

"Stop teasing her, Birdie."

"Then just fucking marry me already, you ass."

He tsks. "I told you, I want the whole shebang. I didn't get that last time. I want this time to be different, special."

"Yeah, yeah." Wren rolls her eyes. "I'm your person and you love me and blah blah romance. Just marry me!"

"Not yet. Calm your tits."

"Foster, man," Winston says, sliding back into the booth after setting two glasses of water on the table. His all-too-familiar scent, the strange combination of bourbon and peppermint, washes over me as he relaxes, spreading his long legs wide, and I feel them brush against mine again. "What'd I say about talking about my sister's tits when I'm around? That's in our agreement."

"I wasn't talking about her *actual* tits," Foster argues.

Wren grabs a boob with each hand, jiggling them. "Good, because these tits cannot be calmed."

"Please stop playing with your boobs in the restaurant," says Simon, the twins' father, shaking his head at his daughter's antics. He shoots me a sweet smile. "Drew, dear, next time you're having car issues, call me."

Dear. Now I know I'm in trouble.

Simon only calls me dear when I've done something he doesn't approve of, which is admittedly more often than I'd like, especially since he's like a second father to me.

Or, well, I guess just a father since mine was never around.

Neither was my mom.

Which is why I find it so laughable that everyone is worried about me not having heat.

Haven't they ever had to live through a winter without so much as an extra blanket and only your hopes and dreams to get you by?

Probably not.

I've been living on the edge of this small beach town for a few years now, and sometimes even I forget the struggles I had to endure growing up, the struggles most people will never even come close to experiencing in their lifetime.

The Daniels family has taken me in like their own to the point that sometimes I forget we're from two completely different worlds.

Theirs is full of love and color.

Mine is full of survival and gray.

It's the reason I hate Winston like I do. He's been handed everything in his life. Everything he's ever wanted, he's gotten. Hell, even when his dad has fired him for being a shitbag, he gets his job back.

Even when he was handed another chance after his accident, he continues to blow it time after time because he can't be bothered to face life head-on. It's like he gave up on himself after the wreck.

Meanwhile I've scratched and clawed my way out of hell just to have what I have now: a broken-down car and a shitty apartment—with no heat, apparently. Both are still better than what I used to have.

Nothing.

Winston wastes the privileges he has in life, and I'd kill for a leg up.

I salute Simon. "Aye aye, sir."

"Don't worry, Pops, I stepped up."

"That's a first," Simon comments.

Winston's bravado falters just a bit, but it's enough for me to notice.

"And, Wren, just let Foster have his big fancy wedding. Stop trying to courthouse-marry the boy."

"See? Even your dad has my back."

"Oh, I think you're stupid as shit for wasting money on a big blowout, but my daughter also needs to learn to…what was it? Calm her tits."

Everyone groans, except Simon, who laughs to himself as he walks away.

"Well, we gotta scram." Foster wraps an arm around his girl's waist. "We have a meeting with a financial planner about getting my landscaping business off the ground, and then we have to go pick up Porter from the airport. It's a busy day."

"I can't believe you're going to be a business owner. It's weird seeing you be so…responsible," Winston remarks.

"It's called growing up, Win. You should try it sometime," Wren tells him.

I see him clench his jaw, but I can't say anything. He's dug his own hole, and now he has to live with the consequences of it.

"What is this—shit on Winston day?"

"As long as they aren't shitting on me anymore. Right, Riker?" I say, tickling him. "As long as they aren't shitting on Mommy, huh? You do that enough for everyone."

He laughs and my heart squeezes at the sound.

Riker might not have been planned, but he's the best unexpected gift I've ever received. I love my son, and I'd do anything for him.

Even accept handouts from someone I despise.

I glance over at Winston and he's watching me play with Riker, a glint of joy in his eyes. Surprising, because all Winston ever looks is bored.

"Pardon me," says Brad, a server here at Slice, as he shoves his way past Wren and Foster. "I have some pie for the lovely new couple."

"For fuck's sake." Winston groans, tossing his head back. "I do one nice fucking thing for someone and I must be sleeping with them? What the hell is wrong with you people?"

"S-Sorry," Brad murmurs. "Simon said you two were together. I-I didn't realize."

Poor Brad.

"My fucking father…" Winston grumbles. "Just leave the pie and get the fuck out of here."

"Winston!" Wren chides. "Thank you, Brad. Sorry about my asshole brother."

Brad scurries off before Winston can yell at him again.

"What are you two doing together today?"

"Couch shopping," I tell her, grabbing for a slice of the breakfast pizza Winston apparently ordered for us.

"Seriously, man? I had to sleep on that fucker for like six months. You sleep on it one goddamn night and you're running out to buy a new one? The fuck, dude?"

Winston lifts a shoulder. "That was your shitty decision."

"I hate you."

"You love me." He takes a bite of his slice of pizza. "Now let me eat my breakfast in peace."

"Real attractive, Win. Mom would be slapping you silly right now if she saw you talking with your mouth full."

He winks at her, not caring.

"Wave bye to your real parents." I grab Riker's hand and shake it at Wren.

"Bye, my sweet boy." She leans down and presses a quick kiss to my cheek. "Good luck with my brother today. Give me a call if you need help burying his body. Foster and I have a contingency plan."

"Wow. So much for being *my* best friend," Winston complains to Foster.

"Hey, man, this one gives me orgasms. I can't say the same for you."

Winston blows him a kiss. "Come here. I'll rock your socks off."

"I doubt you could handle all this."

Wren rolls her eyes, pulling Foster away. "Come on before you strip each other down and get arrested for public indecency."

"You're just jealous he loves me more than he loves you," Winston taunts.

She doesn't respond to him, but Foster throws his best friend a wink.

Idiots.

We're left alone and hit resume on the silence that played between us during the car ride here.

I rock Riker's car seat to keep him entertained and try to scarf down as much food as I can before he inevitably begins to fuss.

"You know you don't have to eat like you're never going to get another meal, right? We can stop for lunch later."

As if on cue, Riker cries.

"Tell that to him." I pull him from his car seat, rocking him in one arm and trying to finish my breakfast at the same time, something I've gotten pretty good at over the last few months.

"You ready to head out?" Winston asks once I finish the slice.

"You mean am I ready to spend the day out and about with you? No, not even close. But since I feel obligated to help you, I'm as ready as I'll ever be."

He doesn't respond to my snark, just slides out of the booth, pulling his leather jacket back over his shoulders and tossing a few bucks down for Brad.

"I'll meet you in the car."

Slice Four

WINSTON

I can pinpoint the exact moment I started hating Drew Woods.

When I met her.

"Are you a virgin?"

I peel my eyes away from the amazing rack I've been admiring for the last few seconds, grinning at the girl glaring back at me. "Excuse me?"

"Well, you're staring at my tits like you're a thirteen-year-old boy who just got his hands on his first nudie mag. So, I repeat: are you a virgin or something? You never seen an actual girl before?"

"You offering to deflower me if I am?"

She throws her head back, laughing so hard the perfect tits I've been staring at bounce.

And bounce and bounce and bounce.

Because she's still fucking laughing at me.

"Oh, god. Thank you for that. I really needed a laugh today."

"Is the thought of having sex with me that hilarious?"

She flicks her eyes up and down my body. "I don't even know you."

I stick my hand out. "Winston Daniels. Nice to meet you…" I trail off, waiting for her to provide her name.

"Daniels? Are you related to Wren?"

I nod, wondering how she knows my sister.

"Then Simon is your dad, right?"

"Yeah…" I draw out. "Who are you again?"

She places her hand in mine. "I'm Drew Woods. Your dad just hired me for the waitressing position."

"What waitressing position? We aren't hiring."

"We are now," my dad interrupts, appearing behind the bar, arms crossed, eyes hard. "Winston, you're fired."

Mouth agape, I glance back at Drew, who is barely holding back her laughter. "Guess I just took your job. Tough luck, virgin."

And just like that, I hated her.

I mean, sure, my dad gave me my job back after two days of begging, but whatever.

The damage was done.

It didn't matter that she had an amazing rack or that her curves were what dreams are made of. It didn't matter that her sharp tongue made me laugh more than it ever hurt me.

I hated her because she was everything I always wanted and nothing I could ever touch. She wouldn't let me get that close; that much was obvious, so I've kept my distance. Played into our game of who can hurt who the most. Let everyone think we're mortal enemies all while I have to talk my dick down any time I'm around her.

I hate Drew Woods.

But not because I don't like her.

I hate her because I do like her…and she won't let me have her.

"There. That should do," Drew says as she arranges the pillows on the couch for the millionth time.

I have no idea how they ended up on my bill, but I'd already swiped my card and the last thing I wanted to do was stand there arguing with the salesperson when there was a screaming baby in my ear, especially after we'd already been there for so many damn hours.

Decorative pillows it is.

"I'm going to go make us some dinner, if that's okay."

"You don't have to ask my permission to eat, Drew."

"You know, I was going to ask if you wanted me to make enough for two but"—she lifts a shoulder—"go fuck yourself."

I bark out a laugh.

Only she would be brave enough to tell the person helping her to go fuck himself.

She flounces out of the room, not a care in the world.

I stare down at the baby sleeping on my brand-new couch, barricaded in with pillows. It's hard for me to fathom how something so sweet could come out of something so sassy.

He looks so tiny, his little hands balled into fists as he snoozes away. His cheeks are chubby, and bright red hair peeks out from under the hood of his polar bear jammies.

Which is odd, because neither his mother nor his shitbag father have red hair.

I would know. I had my fingers tangled in a fistful of it as I held him off the ground.

When I found out how he reacted to Drew being pregnant, never coming around and basically calling her a whore and saying the baby wasn't his behind her back, I didn't waste any time in hunting his ass down and giving him a piece of my mind…and my fist.

"Fine." I snap my eyes Drew's way as she stomps back into the living room. "I'll—" She pauses, her attention dropping to the couch. "You can hold him. If you want to, I mean."

I scoff. "Hold your gremlin who keeps me up all night with his squawking? Did hell freeze over and I missed it?"

"He doesn't even make that much noise," she argues, not the least bit surprised by me not wanting to hold him.

I point to myself. "Light sleeper."

"Whatever." She waves her hand. "I'm making you a sandwich. Not because I like you, but because I feel obligated. Hope you like mustard and mayo."

"What if I don't?"

"Well then tough fucking shit. Dinner will be ready in five. Go wash up."

I tap my temple. "I'll be outside getting my head right."

She sighs but doesn't say anything, heading back into the kitchen as I make my way out the back door.

I grab my trusty box and lighter and take up my usual spot on the deck.

Lighting the joint, I inhale, holding the sweet surrender in my lungs as long as I can as I admire the sea that calls to me like a siren. I itch to go inside and grab my camera to capture the waves in their nighttime essence.

I knew the coast was where I belonged the moment we stepped foot in this town when I was thirteen.

I've been a slave to the waves ever since. They're my favorite thing to photograph.

I suppose it's the one upside to never being able to sleep. Early mornings are my favorite time to catch on film.

"One turkey sandwich and chips," Drew says, sliding a plate down the railing.

"Complete with mayo *and* mustard?"

"Maybe a little something extra."

I grab the sandwich and take a bite. Chew. Swallow. "Yep, hate and discontent. I can taste it."

"Weird. Mine tastes like it was made with love."

"You'd never make anything for me with love. Poison, maybe. Love? Never."

"I think that's a fair assessment."

She grins at me, and we eat our meal in silence.

I stare out at the ocean, and she stares at me.

"What?" I ask when I can't take it anymore, my skin beginning to crawl.

"Nothing."

"Nothing never means *nothing*. What?"

"I'm just trying to figure out your angle here."

I sigh, hating the riddles. "Just tell me what you're trying to say. I'm in no mood for games."

"Why are we here?"

"Because I invited you."

"Why?"

"Because I'm secretly a nice guy."

"Under all that grump? Bullshit."

"Can't you just let it the fuck go and accept it?" I growl.

"Fine. But I'm still suspicious of you."

"Fine."

We resume our silence and I light up my joint again, thinking she'll walk away from the stench of it.

She stays.

"It's beautiful tonight," she comments.

"It really is. Wish I had my camera right now, but I'm too lazy to go grab it."

"You, lazy? Never," she mocks with just enough bitterness in her tone that I can't tell if she's teasing or not. "Do you shoot often?"

"Every morning."

"Seriously?" I don't have to glance at her to know her brows are probably into her hairline. "You get up every morning and take photos?"

"Yep."

I don't elaborate, because it's none of her business what I do in my free time, and because I don't like sharing my hobby with others.

She drops it.

"Does the father ever come around?" I ask, flipping the tables on her as a distraction.

Pot gives me loose lips, and I'd rather not talk about me and start spilling feelings and shit.

"Chadwick?" She wrinkles her nose, frowning. "No. I haven't heard from him since I was three months along. He was half-ass there and then he wasn't there at all. I didn't bother trying to get him involved when it was clear he didn't want to be."

"Did he even reach out when Riker was born?" I take another hit, waiting for her answer.

"Not even a text."

"Is that really a bad thing though?"

She sighs. "I don't know. I mean, on one hand, I'm glad he's not around because I'm so fucking angry at him and the way he reacted when I found out I was pregnant. On the other, I want Riker to have a father figure. I didn't get the chance to grow up with one and look how I turned out."

I huff out a laugh, the smoke trailing around us. "Stubborn. Obnoxious. Strong. Independent. Yeah, those are all real shit qualities to have."

"I'm sorry, did you just say something *nice* about me?"

I point at her. "I called you stubborn and obnoxious too."

"Yeah, but you like me."

"I tolerate you on a good day."

"Uh-huh," she singsongs. "You *like* me."

I take a long step toward her, and because the deck is so small, I can feel her chest brush against mine as her breaths quicken.

She looks so small and fragile staring up at me with big, brown eyes. With the moonlight shining down, they almost look like bourbon.

I fucking *love* bourbon.

Her tongue darts out to wet her lips, and my eyes trace the movement.

She's not like me, just pretending. Drew truly loathes me, and she has no idea she's playing with fire right now.

So, I pull myself back, talking my dick down like I always do. I find the words to throw at her, the ones I know will send her into a rage.

Ones that might even make her laugh.

It's my go-to.

She's a bitch to me, so I'm a dick right back.

It's how we work, how we've always worked.

Why mess up a good thing?

"Like *you*, Drew? No, I don't *like* you. But I do like the way you stare at my cock."

Her mouth drops open and she sputters.

"I-I-I—"

"You what?" I taunt. "You like staring at my cock? Like the way it makes you feel?"

She huffs, rolling her eyes. "Shut up."

"If you ask me nicely, I'll let you touch it."

"Shut the fuck up, Winston!"

"Why?" I laugh again. "Am I hitting too close to your deepest, darkest desires? Do you not hate me as much as you think you do?"

"Oh, I do."

"Then why are your nipples hard right now? Someone like the

idea of touching my cock?"

She glances down. Realizing I'm right, she crosses her arms over her chest, achieving nothing but pushing her tits up higher. "It's just cold out here."

"It's sixty degrees."

"With a breeze," she mumbles quietly, taking a step back, though it doesn't help as much as she hoped. We're still standing close to one another, so close I can smell her pear-scented perfume.

So close I can feel her slide her legs together, trying to relieve the ache building between them.

Drew can hate me all she wants.

But her body doesn't.

"Tell me, Drew, is it really the breeze? Or are you thinking about how good it would feel for me to slide between your legs?"

"Jesus, Winston."

"See? I already have you saying my name twice." I wink.

"Stop it. I don't want to hear any more."

"Why? Because I'm right?"

She snaps her heated gaze toward me, my words having come out harsher than I intended.

"I—"

A high-pitched shriek comes drifting through the open door and both our heads turn toward Riker.

"Move." She shoves at me. "I have to go get my son."

"Saved by the fucking bell," I mutter as she hauls ass past me.

I don't know if I'm referring to her or myself.

Slice Five

DREW

Sleep and I have a precarious relationship that we're barely holding on to.

Some nights, we're grand. Others, we're barely on speaking terms.

Sure, a lot of that has to do with having a new baby, but some nights it's my own mind that keeps me up and worrying all night.

Last night?

That was all Winston's fault.

I couldn't stop thinking about what he said on the patio.

How would it feel for him to slide between my legs?

Judging by the size of his dick, damn good.

The question is…*am I willing to find out?*

I shake my head for likely the millionth time this morning and finish applying my mascara.

I'm already running late for work. I can't dawdle any longer than

I already have or I'll be facing Simon's famous disappointed dad frown. Winston might be used to receiving it, but I sure as hell ain't.

Rushing through the bedroom, I start throwing all of Riker's supplies into his baby bag, knowing if I forget something, Doris probably has a spare at her apartment.

I groan at the thought of having to ask Winston to drive *all* the way across town to drop off Riker, then to work, back over there after work, and then all the way back here.

It's tiresome, especially since we're both working a full day today.

He's going to be nice and bitchy tonight, and I'd rather not upset him any more than I usually do.

"I can watch him, you know."

I squeak at the sudden appearance of Winston's roommate Sully.

We haven't spent too much time together, but what I know of him, I like.

Especially how just being around him eases the anxiety that's always trying to eat at me.

"Uh, Riker?"

"No, Winston." He pushes off the doorjamb and walks into the room, stopping at the edge of the bed. "Yes, Riker. I can watch him for you, if you want. Unless your other sitter lives next door, I'm much more convenient than she is."

I glance down at Riker, who's staring up at Sully like he's the most entertaining thing in the whole world.

Riker does really seem to like him, and he *is* much more convenient than Doris.

"I don't want to put you out or anything..."

"You're not. I offered."

"Are you sure? He cries a lot. And poops."

He chuckles. "I'm well versed in the things babies do. I have two younger siblings I helped raise."

"Really?" Winston appears at the doorway, and I try not to let the same thoughts that plagued me last night rear their ugly heads.

They do anyway.

Because all I can picture is a naked Winston.

A naked Winston crawling on top of me, my legs spread wide as he fits between them like he's always belonged there.

Shit. Shit. Shit.

"I didn't know you had siblings," Winston says.

Right. Siblings. We're having a conversation here.

I pull myself from my fantasies.

Ew—fantasies of Winston? What the hell is wrong with me?

Sully lifts a shoulder. "You never asked."

Winston frowns, and we both ignore him.

"I won't even charge you."

"Like hell you won't," I say. "I'll pay you just as much as I pay Doris. There's no way you're watching my baby for free."

"Why? I'll be home already. Changing a diaper or two and feeding him every so often isn't a big deal."

"Sully…" I shake my head. "Just shut up and let me pay you."

"Whatever." That's all he says before scooping up a smiling Riker like he's done it a million times before and heading toward the living room. "We'll be out here if you need us."

I stare after them, half worried I'm leaving my baby behind with a weirdo and half worried Riker loves Sully more than he loves me.

"He's a really great guy," Winston tells me. "Lay-down-his-life-for-a-stranger kind of great."

"I get that vibe."

"Good. Then chop-chop. We don't want to be late."

"Since when do you care about being on time?"

"Since I don't feel like hearing you bitch at me."

Ah. There he is.

The Winston I needed to get these stupid, juvenile thoughts out of my head.

See? I'm not attracted to him. My hormones are just screwed up after pushing out a baby, and it's been so long since I've had sex that anyone would do at this point.

That's all this is.

It has to be all this is.

I can't possibly be attracted to Winston Daniels.

Hell hasn't frozen over yet.

"Let me just grab my apron and we can go."

He rolls his eyes.

I run into his bathroom one last time, checking to make sure I covered the dark circles under my eyes just enough that nobody is going to ask questions and then snatching my apron off the dresser as I walk back through the bedroom.

I make my way to the living room, smiling when I see Riker sitting with Sully on the couch as *SpongeBob* plays on the TV.

"Can't believe you're letting my kid watch trash cartoons."

"What?" Winston cries. "*SpongeBob* is a classic!"

"I have to agree with him," Sully says.

"He's obnoxious."

"You're obnoxious," Winston grumbles. "Just tell your gremlin goodbye before I leave you here for shitting on my childhood."

I bend to give Riker a kiss and he turns his head into Sully's side.

"If he doesn't want to kiss you, I will."

Sully grins up at me, and I laugh.

Don't get me wrong, Sully is hot as fuck. He looks like your average surfer boy, sun-kissed skin and all, but he doesn't do it for me.

"Fucking move it already," Winston barks from beside the front door, and I glare at him.

"All right. Don't get your panties in a wad. I'm coming."

I follow the grump outside.

Winston grunts and groans his way down the stairs and I want to ask if he's okay, but I'm sure I'll just get a snippy answer back, so I don't bother.

We pile into his old station wagon, complete with the wood paneling.

"This is such an odd choice in vehicle for you," I comment as he cranks the engine, which sounds surprisingly good for such an old car.

"It was my parents'."

"No way. I thought for sure it was brand new."

He ignores my snark. "I have a lot of good memories in this beast, so I couldn't let her go when my mom passed. My dad was ready to sell her, but I vowed to keep her alive and well."

"She's in great condition."

"Not too bad, especially considering this is what I was driving when I got hit."

Ah, yes. The accident no one likes to talk about.

It happened right after I moved here. Although I didn't know him all that well at the time, I knew him well enough to gather that the Winston after the accident was a lot different than the one I met before it.

Still a jerk, but way viler.

His words burned where they used to sting.

He was so angry, so full of hate.

I tried not to take it personally, but if I'm being honest, I did.

I think the thing I hated most about the entire thing was that even though he could have lost his life, he still treated it like it was something to sneeze at, like the privileges he had were meaningless.

He didn't show any respect for himself or others around him. He just kept existing, not caring about who he hurt along the way.

He lights a cigarette, balancing it between his lips as he holds the wheel with one hand and cranks the window down with the other.

I know smoking isn't sexy, but damn does he look it with his arm resting on the door panel, smoke wafting around him. The muscles in his arms jump as he lifts the cigarette to his mouth and takes a drag, and I watch with rapt attention.

"Do you want one?"

I gulp. "H-Huh?"

"A smoke—do you want one? You keep staring at me like you do."

That's not what I want.

I clear my throat and move my attention to the road. "I don't smoke."

"Right." He takes another drag.

The drive to Slice isn't long, and thankfully we pull into the parking lot just before I do something stupid.

Like moan and say I wish I were the cigarette.

I push the door open before I even know the car is in park and hightail it toward the front door.

I swear I hear Winston laugh behind me.

I'm in such a rush I nearly crash right into Simon as I burst through the pizzeria doors.

"Whoa, Speed Racer! What's the rush? That excited to sling pizzas?"

"I'd be more excited if I were in the kitchen," I say, giving him my sweetest smile.

He chuckles. "Tell ya what—if anyone calls in this week, I'll let you stand in on the prep station. Deal?"

"Prep station?" I groan because I don't want to just work prep. I want to create.

Simon raises his brows, and I know I'm pushing my luck complaining when he's being so generous.

"Deal." I push my shoulders back. "That's what I meant to say. You have a deal."

"Good. Now go clock in."

He turns on his heel and I clear my throat before he can get far.

He spins back around to me with a questioning glance. "Yes?"

I stick my hand out. "Shake on it?"

Laughing and shaking his head, he clasps my hand in his. "Smart girl."

Winston finally ambles inside, clapping his dad on the back. "What's up, Dad?"

Simon checks the watch on his wrist. "Well, I'll be damned. You're on time."

"You have me to thank for that."

"Pfft," Winston scoffs. "You almost made us late with all your diddle-daddling."

"I was saying goodbye to my child."

"Excuses, excuses."

Simon smacks the back of Winston's head. "Shut up. Go clock in and do something with your life."

Winston glares at me, rubbing his head.

I just stick my tongue out and head for the computer so I can get paid for having to deal with Winston all night long.

Once I'm on the clock, I tie my apron around my waist and head for my first table, pasting on my customer service smile.

"Welcome to Slice. What can I—oh, it's just you."

Wren and Foster grin up at me.

"Just us?" Wren pouts. "You hear that, Foster? It's *just us*."

"Ignore her," Foster says. "She's insane today."

"To be fair, she's insane every day."

The guy sitting next to Foster laughs. "I like her. Is she single?"

I look him over, his dark blond hair perfectly coifed and his skin a rich tan. His eyes are dark green, smile bright white.

Is there something in the water around here? Because all the guys are stupid hot.

"Why don't you ask her yourself?" I say.

He whistles. "Damn. Yeah, I *really* like you." He sticks his hand out across the table. "I'm Porter. And you are…?"

"Single."

"Drew!" Wren laughs.

"What? I am."

"You're horrible."

"She's hot."

"She's insufferable."

I sigh, because *of course* Winston must butt into this conversation at this exact moment.

"Go away, Winston," Wren tells her brother. "You're not wanted here."

"I am too." He looks to Foster. "Right, best friend?"

"Oooh." I clap my hands together. "The decision between free pussy and dealing with a butthurt Winston—let's definitely play this game."

"Where do I play into all of this?" Porter tosses his hat into the ring.

Everyone stares at Foster expectantly.

His eyes bounce from face to face, gulping nervously.

"I…I like everyone equally?"

He says it as a cautious question like the smart man he is.

"But me just a little bit more, right? Because you've known me the longest and all," Winston throws out.

"Or, you know, me the most because of that free pussy thing," Wren says.

"Ew." Winston groans. "Stop talking about your nasty vagina."

"Actually"—Foster holds his finger up—"it's not nasty. Can confirm that one.'"

Winston gags, and we all laugh at him.

"There we have it. I'm the clear victor." Wren pats herself on the back. "Thank you, thank you. I'll accept chocolate in lieu of congratulations." She looks pointedly at Foster when she says this.

"Noted," he tells her, winking.

"Do you guys know what you want? Or did you need a minute?" I ask.

"I want the Grilled Cheese Cheeser for sure," Wren says. "And some breadsticks."

"Naturally," I say. "For you, Porter?"

"I'll do a slice of what she got and one of the Biscuit 'N' All the Gravy too. And then can I have a kids-sized slice of the Mac 'N' Cheese, Please pizza."

"Kids-sized?" I scrunch my brows. "You sure you don't just want a regular slice? It's really good and totally worth the extra calories."

Porter points to the other side of the booth, and for the first time, I notice the little girl who is completely zonked out.

Her hair—which is the exact same color as her father's—is pulled into a lopsided top knot, her lashes so long against her tan cheeks.

"It's for my daughter."

"Oh." It comes out a whisper, like we haven't all been talking in normal voices for the past five minutes. "I didn't even see her there."

"She's a little bitty thing," he says. "She hides easily."

I grin down at her. "She's precious."

Wren snaps her fingers together. "Shit! Why didn't I think to ask you before? Drew, who is the lady you have watch Riker?"

"Lady? Don't you mean little girl? She's like sixteen or some shit," Winston interjects.

"Who, Doris? She isn't sixteen. She's nineteen. She's in

community college." I look to Porter. "Do you need a sitter?"

He nods. "Not yet, but I will eventually. Someone able to be a live-in nanny would be ideal."

I'm not sure Doris would be up for a live-in nanny position, but I do know she could really use a better place to live and more stable income. No harm in throwing her info out there just in case.

"I can have a talk with her and give you her number. She's fantastic with my three-month-old. I bet she'd love to help you out."

"Thank you, I appreciate it."

I smile at him. "It's no problem. I'll be right back with some waters for you guys."

"Hey, what about my order?" Foster asks.

"Please. I already know your dumb ass wants chicken strips."

"Really, man? You order chicken strips at a pizzeria?" Porter chides. "Fine, Winston, you win. I don't want his best friend status anymore."

Winston fist-pumps the air. "Yes!"

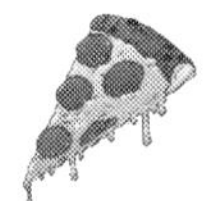

"I am fucking beat," I grumble as Winston pulls the station wagon into his driveaway. "Is it wrong if I want my child to be soundly sleeping when we walk inside?"

"Nah."

He reaches across the front seat and I hear a loud crackle come from his shoulder that I'm sure can't be normal. Again, I keep quiet as he pops open the glove compartment, grabbing a box.

"Matter of fact," he says, clicking it open, "we're going to pretend we aren't even here yet."

He rolls the window down and lights up a joint, puffing on it for several moments before saying anything.

"I can feel you judging me."

"I'm not judging you," I tell him. "I just don't get it."

"Get what?"

"Why you smoke that."

"Do you have a problem with it?"

"No. I used to smoke when I was a teen, but that was a long damn time ago."

"Really?" He looks at me, brows raised with a mocking grin. "Now that bit of information is surprising."

"If you think that's surprising, I better never tell you about the rest of my childhood and teenage years."

"What? Did you not get straight As because you smoked a little pot?"

"Straight As?" I scoff. "I barely graduated high school with how much we bounced around. I went to seven different schools in four years. We didn't live anywhere long enough for me to ever settle in."

He doesn't say anything, just watches me and takes another hit.

"What? Did you think I grew up with a white picket fence? Think again, Winston."

He accused me of judging him just moments ago, and now he's the one judging me. I look away from him, because I can't stand his curious eyes boring into me.

"I've just never seen anything good come from it with other people who use it like you do," I say to him.

"People like me?"

"Yeah, the ones chasing something."

"What the hell is that supposed to mean?"

"It means you don't smoke for fun, Winston. You use it as a way to chase your demons away. You smoke to feel nothing."

He gives me a derisive laugh. "You're wrong there."

"Oh yeah?" I cross my arms, dying to know how that's possible. "How so?"

"I don't smoke to feel nothing, Drew. I smoke to feel everything."

Before I can say anything else, he's out of the car and stomping off inside.

With a reluctant sigh, because a bitchy Winston is so not what I wanted to deal with tonight after the long day I had, I follow him inside.

My prayers have been answered because Riker is out cold when I check on him in Sully's room.

"He's good. We're good. Just get a good night's sleep," the surfer tells me, waving me away as he types a million miles an hour on his keyboard.

Normally, I'd argue with him, because he's my baby and my responsibility.

But tonight I'm worn out to the bone and a night off sounds amazing.

As I retreat to Winston's room, heading straight for the shower because I need to scrub this day away, I see him standing out on the patio, smoke swirling around him.

I briefly wonder if it's pot or a cigarette this time and what it is he's running from.

Winston has the perfect life. Everything he wants is at his fingertips. He survived a horrible accident with no permanent damage, and with the settlement he got, he bought his house. He doesn't even have to work full-time to keep up with his bills. He can literally just sit around, surf, and do photography on the side whenever his hands itch to hold his camera.

In my eyes, he has it made.

Whatever he's chasing—either something or nothing—I don't understand it one bit.

I leave the bedroom door open a crack just in case Sully needs me and then I strip off my work outfit, grateful to remove the pizza-smell-infused material.

I turn the water up as hot as I can stand it and release an audible sigh when the stream cascades over my tired body.

This is what I've been looking forward to all damn day.

Hell, maybe even all week.

Or month.

No. *Definitely* for the last three months, since before my life changed drastically.

Don't get me wrong, I knew when I was all swollen and pregnant that my life as I knew it was over. I knew I'd probably never again feel the joy of a full night of sleep, knew I'd probably never pee in peace again and wouldn't ever be able to eat a meal with two hands, no matter how quickly I could shovel the food into my mouth.

What I wasn't planning on was never having a full moment to myself ever again.

Even when I'm not with Riker, I'm thinking about him, thinking about what I need to do to provide for him, for his future.

I think about him all the time.

Even now, when I know he's in the capable hands of Sully the child whisperer, I'm worried about him waking up in the middle of the night. What if he misses me? What if he needs me?

Sighing, I lather the soap through my hair then grab my razor so I can shave my legs for the first time in way too long.

All the while, I try to push thoughts of Riker away and just enjoy the night Sully is giving me without letting my second best friend creep into my mind.

Mommy guilt.

It's the main reason I'm constantly worrying about Riker.

If I don't worry about it, it means I don't love him as much as I possibly can. It means I'm doing something wrong. It means I'm not being the best mom I can be.

Or at least that's what my brain tells me.

"I can hear you thinking in there."

I scream, the razor in my hand slicing into my leg. I feel the sting of the water hitting the wound before I can see the blood begin to gather. "SON OF… CHRIST ON A CRACKER, WINSTON! What the fuck are you doing in here?"

He sighs. "Do we really have to go over how this is *my* bathroom again? I'm brushing my teeth so I can try to sleep through your snoring."

I poke my head around the shower curtain and throw a shampoo bottle at him.

"Hey, watch it! You could have hit me in the face. How would you feel if I choked on my own toothbrush?"

"I'd think it was fitting, and deserved since I am *clearly* taking a shower. Don't you know what fucking boundaries are?"

"Again, *my* bathroom."

"I just cut my leg because you scared the shit out of me!" I say, ignoring his interruption. "Go get me some Band-Aids, dammit!"

Winston groans, but I can hear him stomp out of the bathroom.

I quickly finish shaving my leg and run my loofa over my body, trying to beat Winston in his hunt so I'm not naked when he comes back in.

I'm out of the shower, just tucking my towel into place when he comes barreling back through the door, a small box in hand.

"Took me forever to find these. Here's your bitch stickers."

"Bitch stickers?"

"Yeah. Only little bitches use Band-Aids."

"Then why are they Ninja Turtle themed? Kinda cutesy for a guy who never uses them."

"Because my sister is a brat and bought them for me as a housewarming gift."

"What a convenient cover story."

"They've sat unopened for years," he maintains. "They're probably expired."

"Band-Aids don't expire," I mutter, rolling my eyes. "Thanks. You can go now."

Only he doesn't move.

His bright blue eyes roam over my body.

His gaze feels like fire has licked its way beneath my towel, sneaking into all the spaces I will never tell anyone I imagine him sliding into.

I don't know if it's the residual steam from my hot shower or his gaze, but the longer I stand here, the more I want to jump back in the stall and crank the water to cold to soothe this burn.

I can't recall the last time someone looked at me like this.

Like I was something special.

Something desirable.

Worthy.

He takes a step toward me, and it pulls me from my haze.

I'm tired. I'm not thinking straight.

This is *Winston* for crying out loud.

"See something you like?" I say to break the tension.

I watch as my words work their way through his head.

First his eyes meet mine. Then brows scrunch together. Lips pull into a sneer.

"Nah. Just trying to figure out why you're bothering wasting your time shaving your legs. Not like anyone is going to want to fuck you now that you have baby baggage attached."

Winston's fist sinks into my stomach.

Or at least that's what his words feel like.

Forget the cold shower. His comments are icy enough to cool anyone off.

I try to straighten my shoulders, try not to let it show just how deep his words cut.

I try not to cry, especially in front of him.

"Odd since you're the one standing there with a half-hard dick, so clearly turned on by my baby-baggage body."

I don't know if that's true. I didn't look. I refuse to look.

"Here's your fucking Band-Aids."

He tosses the box onto the counter, leaving in a huff.

I breathe a sigh of relief when the door clicks closed.

Then I reach for the faucet handles, hoping the sound of the water will drown out my cries.

Slice Six

WINSTON

Drew and Riker have been staying with me for just over a week.

And three days have passed since we last spoke outside of work.

I've barely slept. Have had little to no appetite. I haven't even had the desire to smoke.

Nothing is making me feel good.

The worst part is that it's no one's fault but my own.

I should have never said what I said to Drew. She's barely even glanced at me since I told her nobody would want to sleep with her now that she has a baby.

That's a complete and total fucking lie.

After seeing her in a towel, I spent half the night with a throbbing cock. I waited for Drew to fall asleep before I snuck back into my bathroom to shower just so I could relieve myself.

Now every time I see her, I feel guilty.

Not for jacking off to her, because I'm a grown-ass man and I accept my actions.

But because every time I look at her, she appears so…dejected, and I know that's all my fault.

My eyes drift toward the back patio for probably the twentieth time in the last ten minutes.

We're both off today and Drew is out back with Riker, laughing at him as he plays in his little chair. It's the only time she looks happy, when she's with her son.

I shift my attention back to my laptop. I'm working on editing a few photos I took of the ocean last night.

I don't know why I bother editing anything I upload onto my hard drive. It's not like it's going anywhere. I don't share my photography with anyone outside of my family.

I don't shoot for money. I shoot for me. I enjoy it too much to put the pressure on myself to turn it into anything more than a hobby.

I know me better than that.

Drew lets out a loud laugh, and my eyes drift back to hers because I can't seem to stop them from seeking her out.

She's cracking up at something Riker's done, and her smile is infectious, even when it's not aimed at me.

I don't realize I've set my laptop aside and picked up my camera until I hear the familiar shutter sound—and feel the recognizable ache in my shoulder.

It's getting harder and harder to hold it steady.

How the fuck can holding a camera hurt so badly?

Probably because you're a dumbass and didn't complete physical therapy.

Ignoring the pain, I snap a few photos of Drew and Riker, knowing she'll appreciate mementos of these little moments with her son when she's less angry at me.

I pop the memory card out and start uploading the images to the computer, saving them to the folder I created just for her.

It's not a creepy folder or my spank bank.

When Drew isn't looking, I've been taking pictures of her and Riker.

Or just her.

I remember when my mother died, and we had to go through our box of pictures for her memorial service. We had such a difficult time finding ones with my mom in them, as she was always the one behind the camera. She was the one waiting on the shoreline, ready to feed us or reapply sunscreen. She was the one sitting off to the side capturing the moments on film as my dad played baseball with us around the yard.

She was in on the action, but there's nothing to prove it.

Going through that box made me realize that any time she sat down to look through old photos, she never saw herself with us.

I don't want that for anyone else.

"NOOOO!"

A loud screech filters through the sliding glass door and I leap up, rushing toward Drew before I can even think twice.

"Move, move, move!" she shouts as she comes barreling in, holding Riker away from her. "Shit, shit, shit!"

"Literal or metaphorical shit?"

"Metaphorical!" she hollers as she rushes past me and into my bedroom. I follow her. "He projectile vomited all over himself and me. Can you grab the basket from the laundry room?"

I spring into action, racing to grab what she needs.

When I skid back into my bedroom, Riker is pissed. His little scrunched-up face is beet red and his lungs are at their max capacity.

"Here." I toss the basket onto the bed.

"No! No, no, no," Drew chants as she digs through it. "I didn't change the load over. Fuck!"

"What's wrong?"

"This isn't my stuff, it's Sully's. I'm out of clean burp rags *and* shirts for myself."

She's been running this operation we have going on with limited supplies. It wasn't such a huge issue when she was taking Riker to Doris because she has her own hoard of baby essentials, but now that Sully seems to have taken over babysitting duties most days, it's clear we're running extremely low on things.

"It's fine. I'll go grab a towel."

I scamper out of the room, snatching one from the top of the linen closet and beating feet back to my bedroom to try to help Drew in any way I can.

She's so close to her breaking point, I can see it.

Riker is still going nuts, and all I want to do is relieve some of the pressure she's feeling.

I come to a halt when I enter the bedroom.

Drew's standing with a crying, almost-naked Riker on her hip.

Shirtless.

If I thought Drew Woods in an old, shabby green towel was prime jack-off material, I was wrong.

It's this moment right here.

Not because she's topless, though that isn't hurting anything at all.

It's not her appearance, because let's face it, her eyes are sunken from lack of sleep and her hair is an awful mess.

It's none of that.

It's the way she looks at her son, even as he cries so loudly my eardrums are hurting.

The way she took the literal shirt off her back just to clean him up so he's not sitting there soaked in his own spit-up.

The way she's singing off-key.

The way she's dancing to no music.

It's just…her.

She's breathtaking.

Drew gets Riker to latch on to the binky she's holding, he finally begins to quiet down, and relief floods her face.

"Oh, thank god." She sighs. "I thought he would never stop."

She stands there, rocking him for several more minutes until his tired eyes grow heavy. Placing him on the bed with what I'm sure is all the gentleness she can muster, she tucks his blanket around him and backs away slowly, hoping he'll fall for it and take a nap, or at least let her clean up without screaming.

When she's sure he's not going to freak out again, she stands.

Hands on her hips, eyes closed, she tilts her face skyward, muttering something I can't make out.

I take the opportunity to look her over.

I always thought Drew was attractive. The first time we met, she caught me staring at her rack, so it's no secret I'm physically attracted to her.

But since having Riker, her body has transformed in subtle, sexy ways.

Her hips are wider, fuller. Still flat, her stomach has a squishiness to it that wasn't there before—and I would know because the girl *loves* her belly shirts. Her tits aren't as perky and perfect as they once were, giving them a more natural look.

She's sexier than she's ever been.

As if she can feel my eyes on her, she slides her tired gaze to me.

"What the fuck are you looking at?" she snaps, curling her arm around her waist.

I want to march over there and peel it away.

How fucking dare she cover her perfect body up. How dare she act like she's anything less than gorgeous.

But it's not my place to say anything to her.

So I gnash my teeth together, yank the tee I'm wearing over my head, and toss it her way. "Here. A clean shirt."

She catches it, staring at the object like it's foreign for a moment before, much to my surprise, she slides the material over her head without any argument.

It's way too big on her and she looks ridiculous in it, but I can tell she's relieved to be covered up.

"Thanks." She lets out a groan. "Sorry, that was an intense few minutes there."

"It's not a problem."

"Really? All my…what was it?" She taps her finger to her chin. "Ah yes, I remember." She crosses her arms over her chest, her signature *I'm fucking pissed* stance. "Baby baggage, right? My baby baggage isn't an issue for you?"

I wince, loathing having my words thrown back at me. "Fuck, Drew. I didn't mean it. I was—"

She holds her hand up. "You know what, Winston? Save it. I'm tired of hearing your excuses. Besides"—she lifts a shoulder—"I'm used to you talking to me like I'm trash. Nothing new."

I feel like I've been run over by a truck.

And it must be exactly how Drew felt the other night when I spouted off the most bullshit thing ever.

"Drew—"

"No, really, Winston. It's fine. *I'm* fine. Like I said, totally used to it. You always say mean things to me. It's how our relationship works."

"You say mean things to me too."

"But I don't ever mean them. I don't ever say things to cut at you. I say things in jest."

"I *didn't* mean it," I insist, crossing the room and standing before her, trying to make her *see* how sorry I am. "I was just high and I always say stupid shit when I'm high. I can't handle my emotions all that well when the pot kicks in."

She laughs sardonically. "Right. Blame the weed, Win. That's really grown up of you. It's the same shit my mom used to do when she'd shoot up. She didn't pay the bills on time because she was too high. She didn't buy groceries because the 'good stuff' made her forget. She didn't pick me up from school because the dope made her too tired. It's just an excuse like she used to make." She steps closer to me and her eyes darken so much they almost look black even from this close. "Face it, Winston—you didn't say it because you were high. You said it because you're a prick."

I grab her wrist when she spins on her heel, not letting her get far.

She peers up into my eyes, still looking hurt and angry, and I try to convey with my own that I never meant to hurt her.

"I'm sorry, Drew. I'm sorry, okay?"

"Like I said, Winston, I'm used to it."

She yanks her arm back, and I let her walk away.

"You have to be fucking kidding me."

I roll over on the couch, blindly reaching for my phone on the coffee table.

12:13AM.

Riker's crying.

Again.

Not long after Drew walked away from me, Riker woke up, lungs ready for another screaming match.

He's cried. Drew's cried. And I'm about to fucking cry because all I want to do is sleep and I can't.

I passed on the pot tonight, taking what Drew said earlier seriously.

Maybe she's right. Maybe I am just a prick, but the pot doesn't help. Sure, it helps me feel calm inside, but it's just a Band-Aid.

Pot is my bitch sticker.

And I'm no bitch.

I lie here for a few minutes, waiting for the familiar *Shh, it's okay*, but I don't hear Drew shuffle around.

I pull myself off the couch and make my way to my bedroom.

Drew is out cold, sprawled across one half of the bed, the fatigue having set in completely. Riker, who is usually blocked in on the bed with a fort of pillows, is nowhere to be seen.

I follow the sounds of the crying to the other side of the bed, and I'm surprised to find him swaddled in a blanket lying inside one of my dresser drawers on the floor.

"What the…"

Without a second thought, I bend down and scoop him up out of the drawer, cuddling him close to my chest.

He's so tiny in my hands.

Warm and fragile.

An overwhelming sense of protectiveness falls over me, and I cup my hand around his little body like I can safeguard him from all the dangers in the world.

"Shh, it's okay," I tell him, just like Drew always does, bouncing him up and down a few times and ignoring the stabbing in my shoulder. "I've got ya, buddy. It's okay."

To my surprise, he begins to quiet down, nuzzling his face into my chest like this is exactly where he wanted to be all along.

I glance down at the bed, which looks incredibly inviting.

Sure, the new couch I bought is a million times better than the old one, but I miss my bed, and if I'm not smoking tonight, I'm at least going to be comfortable.

Slipping into the bed as smoothly as I can manage, I make myself comfortable and get Riker situated—complete with his pillow fort—between me and Drew.

I get the binky back into Riker's mouth, patting his belly. "You're all good now, little man. Nice and comfy up here. Go back to sleep for your mama."

As if on cue, Drew stirs, and I slam my eyes closed because if I can't see her, she can't see me.

The logic of a fucking child.

"What's going on?" she mutters. "What happened? Is he okay?"

I peel my eyes open. "He was fussing, so I figured I'd come in and help."

"He was?" She rubs at her face. "Shit, I didn't even hear him. I'm so fucking tired."

"It's fine," I tell her. "Just go back to sleep. He's good now."

She looks down between us, her eyes quickly going to where Riker's tiny fist is wrapped around my finger. He's made it clear I'm not going anywhere tonight.

"He's so perfect," she whispers.

"He's okay," I say.

She chuckles, falling back onto the bed with a sigh. "I can't believe I didn't hear him."

"I have no idea how you slept through it. He woke me up from the living room. Well, not like that's saying much. I don't sleep very well, especially if I don't smoke."

She twists her head toward me when I confess this, but she doesn't say anything.

"Why was Riker in my dresser drawer?"

Shrugging, she says, "He sleeps in one at my apartment. I just figured he was missing it and put him in one tonight when he wouldn't fall asleep. I'll put everything back together in the morning."

"Your kid sleeps in a drawer?"

"It's cheaper than a crib. I'm not rolling in dough, in case you didn't notice."

I don't say anything, because we both know the gravity of her situation.

"You don't have to stay in here," she says after several beats of silence play between us.

As if he can understand her, Riker begins to fuss again.

"Okay, okay." She rubs his head. "I was kidding. He can stay, just as long as he doesn't try to feel me up or anything."

"Please. You're the one who creeps on people when they're changing."

"I did not creep!" she whisper-shouts. "You were changing with the door open!"

"My bathroom."

She sighs. "Shut up."

"Admit it, Drew—I make you hot."

"Moister than a fucking oyster," she says dryly, closing her eyes.

I laugh and she swats at me. "Ouch. What was that for?"

"You're going to wake the baby with all that shaking, and I will *not* help you get him back to sleep if you do that."

"I don't need your help. He clearly likes me."

"He's the only one," she complains. "Go to bed, Winston."

Grinning, I close my eyes, because I know she's wrong.

Drew does like me.

Maybe not right now, but I know deep down she does on some level. If she didn't, she wouldn't be so worried about the reasons I smoke.

In her own way, Drew cares about me.

And I care about her too.

"Hey, Drew?"

"Oh my god. Can't you be quiet for two seconds?"

"This is important."

She rolls onto her side, glaring at me. "What," she mutters, grinding her teeth.

"I don't think you have to worry about anyone not wanting to sleep with you because of your baby."

"I was totally kidding about being moister than an oyster. I'm dryer than the Sahara right now. Quit hitting on me."

I laugh again. "I'm being serious."

"I am too. I'm tired. I'm not horny."

"Drew!"

She smirks at me. "I know you're sorry, Win. But I'm still mad, okay? Your words hurt me, even if you didn't mean them. They're real fears I have, and I didn't care for hearing them spoken out loud."

On one hand, her words elate me. She hasn't outright forgiven me, but she's not *not* forgiving me either. That's a step in the right direction.

But on the other hand…god, it makes me feel like complete shit.

Does she really feel that way? That nobody is going to want her because she's a single mom? Does she really expect to be alone the rest of her life?

Maybe I'm just interpreting her words wrong…

"You really think no one is going to want you because you have a baby?"

"Uh, yeah," she says like she's being completely logical right now when she sounds insane. "A baby is a big fucking responsibility. There aren't many people out there who are going to want to take that on."

I would.

The thought hits me out of nowhere.

Would I really do that for Drew? For Riker? Would I step up and take care of them both even though they don't belong to me?

Yes.

The weirdest part of all? Wanting to take care of them doesn't scare me.

It feels…right, and not just in a *Wow, what a good dude doing a good deed* kind of way.

It's more than that.

It's them.

I've never wanted kids. They're loud and needy and I like my sleep—whenever I can get it—and my freedom way too much to be saddled with a child.

But that doesn't mean if the right someone came along and wanted kids—or had their own—I would run the other way. I would make it work. I would find a way to get over my preconceived notions and make it work.

That's the way I'm feeling right now, like I'd find a way with Drew and Riker.

"Shit," she continues. "Not even Chadwick wanted me, and Riker is his baby for crying out loud."

I sneer. Just thinking of the jackass makes my blood boil. "Please. Chadwick is a tool with the worst name in the history of names. He's an ass and by no means who you should be basing your future love life off. Fuck that guy."

"I did, and look where it got me."

I don't laugh at her joke, because I hate the idea of someone else touching her.

Especially someone who doesn't deserve her.

"For the record, I think you're insane."

"For the record," she mocks, "I don't care what you think. I just want to go to sleep."

"Fine." I roll onto my back.

"Fine."

"Good night, Drew."

She grunts again, kicking her feet like a kid throwing a fit. "Always have to have the last word, don't you? Good night, Winston."

I open my mouth.

"Don't you dare say another word!" she warns. "Go. The fuck. To sleep."

"That's the name of my favorite children's book."

"You would read children's books, since you're a giant baby and all."

"You're mean when you're tired."

"Just when I'm tired?" She smiles sweetly. "Sleep, Winston."

"Yes, ma'am."

Chuckling to myself, I close my eyes.

And I fall asleep faster than I have in a long damn time.

DREW

Daylight drifts in through Winston's curtains, and I swear in that moment that, to pay him back for allowing me to stay here, the second I get any spare cash, I'm buying him blackout curtains.

If it wasn't for the damn sun blinding me, I'd still be sleeping peacefully. And truth be told, that was the best night of sleep I've had in a long damn time.

I peel my eyes open and glance across the sleeping baby to the other side of the bed.

It's empty.

"Of course he's gone," I say aloud.

Disappointment hits me like a ton of bricks. It's not like I expected us to stay in bed all day or anything. Winston isn't *mine* to do that with, but…

I thought maybe after his moment of vulnerability last night, he wouldn't be so closed off and we'd…well, I don't know what I wanted exactly.

I just know I didn't want him to be gone.

My alarm sounds and I reach for my cell on the bedside table, silencing it before it wakes Riker.

I roll over to wake my baby, only my hand hits an empty bundle of blankets.

What the…

I spring from the bed, racing around the other side to check the drawer.

Maybe last night was all a dream. Maybe Winston never came in.

Except Riker isn't there either.

"Son of a…"

I sprint from the room, taking off down the hall to Sully's bedroom.

Nothing.

The panic sets in.

I charge through the house, searching every room, but I keep turning up empty.

"My son is gone. Where the fuck is my son? Where is my baby?! Where—"

I hear his giggle and my eyes fly to the back patio I've passed so many times in my pursuit.

Riker is sitting comfortable in Sully's arms as they watch the waves play along the shoreline.

I breathe a sigh of relief and make my way out to them.

"Sullivan Insert-Your-Last-Name-Here, you scared the shit out of me."

Sully turns around, grinning at me. "Oops." He bounces Riker. "Say, 'Sorry, Mama. We just wanted to let you sleep in.'"

I pinch at Riker's cheeks and he coos at me. "You scared me half to death, you little turkey."

"Scott," Sully says. "My last name is Scott."

"Sullivan Scott." I smile softly. "I like it."

He shrugs. "It's a name."

There's something in the way he says it, like he doesn't love or hate it. He's resigned to it.

Huh.

I brush it off. If Sully wants to talk, he'll talk.

"When did he wake up?"

"I heard him about an hour ago."

"I can't believe I slept through him waking up twice."

"Eh, you were tired, and you knew we'd take care of him."

I grab Riker from Sully's arm, giving him a kiss. "Is this what it's like to have a partner? You get to sleep in occasionally and don't have to worry every second of every day?"

"I don't know about the worrying part." Sully rubs at the back of his neck. "But I'm sure it makes everything else just a little bit easier."

"Well, thank you. I appreciate it."

"It's no problem. He's a good kid."

"You keep taking such good care of my son and I'll propose marriage. Wait!" I gasp. "Crazy idea here, but let's run off and get married. You're single, I'm single, Riker loves you—let's do it."

Sully laughs. "I don't think Winston would be too fond of that idea."

"Who gives a rat's ass what he thinks? He doesn't even like me."

He grunts but doesn't say anything else.

"Where is Winston anyway? I have to be at work within the hour."

"He said he was going to the store, but that was a while ago. Do you need me to drive you?"

"No." I sigh. "I can take the bus. This whole not-having-a-car thing is getting really old."

"Do you know when it'll be fixed?" He holds his hands up. "Not that I don't like having you and my buddy here. I'm just wondering for your sanity."

"You know, I'm not entirely sure. Winston set something up with Mr. Schwartz and said it would probably be a week, but we're past that now. He hasn't brought up that it's ready, so I haven't asked. Maybe I should."

He nods. "Not a bad idea. We both know how…forgetful Winston can be."

"You mean lazy. You can call him what he is around me. I don't mind one bit."

Sully chuckles. "I don't think he's always what he seems to be."

I scrunch my brows. "You doing that hippie bullshit again?" I look down at Riker. "Oh god, you didn't turn my baby into a hippie too, did you?"

Grinning, he shakes his head. "I'm just saying Winston's an interesting guy. I've been living with him for a while now and he's not always the lazy shithead he seems to be."

"I'll take your word for it." I adjust Riker in my arms. "All right. I gotta go get ready for work so I can get him settled and catch the bus."

"Here, let me have him. You go get ready."

"Sully, I can't have you watching my child all the time. It doesn't feel right."

"If I had a problem with it, I wouldn't offer. Besides, I miss my siblings. It's like having them around again. And it gets lonely here during the day."

"Do you not work?"

He gives me a *You serious?* look. "Of course I work. I'm just off for the winter."

"What?"

"I help run a fishing boat and we're in the off-season."

"You help run a fishing boat? How did I not know that about you?"

He shrugs. "I don't know. I don't talk about it much, and we don't exactly hang out like best buddies."

"True. Okay, fine." I hold Riker out to him. "He's all yours then. I'm gonna run inside and get ready, then I'll be out for goodbyes."

Sully holds Riker up. "Wanna go watch *SpongeBob* with Uncle Sully?"

Riker grins then pukes all over him.

"Welcome to the joys of parenting!" I laugh, giving him a finger wave. "Toodles!"

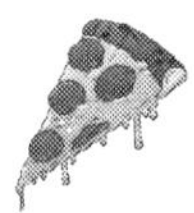

I set Sully up with everything he'd need, kissed Riker goodbye, and booked it out the door so I could make the city bus on time.

"Come on, come on," I mutter as the people in front of me dawdle their way off the bus in the slowest possible fashion.

Getting off at my stop, I race down the sidewalk, hook a right, and practically sprint the rest of the three blocks, trying frantically to beat the clock.

I wasn't late a single time when I was pregnant and not even the first week I was back to work after I had Riker.

I'll be damned if I'm late now because of Winston.

Simon's standing behind the counter when I make it to Slice with just a minute to spare before my clock-in time.

"You're late."

"I still have one minute!" I insist.

"Please don't tell me Winston's rubbing off on you."

"Ew, Dad. Don't talk about Winston rubbing *anything* off."

Simon shakes his head at his daughter as she slides up to the counter. "Where did I go wrong with you?"

"Wrong…or right?" she teases.

"Anything open in the kitchen today?" I ask Simon before he takes off.

"Depends. Do you wanna make tips or wash dishes?"

I wrinkle my nose. "Tips sound good."

"That's what I thought." He laughs, tossing a dishrag over his shoulder. "By the way, now you're late."

"Shit!" I race to the computer and punch myself in.

"Shame my big brother is such a bad influence on you." Wren frowns. "I thought you were better than that."

"Shut it, Birdie."

"Hey! You can't call me that."

"I'll do as I please." I wrap my apron around my waist, expertly tying it behind my back. "What are you doing here anyway? I thought last week was your final shift."

"Dad needed an extra hand after Winston called in."

"He called in?"

"Did he not say anything to you?"

I shake my head. "No. He was gone when I rolled over this morning. He—"

I realize what I've said too late.

Wren's brows are nearing her hairline and her lips are curved into a wide grin. "Well, well, well. What an interesting tidbit."

"It's not what it sounds like," I tell her. "I promise."

"Are you sure about that?"

"Do I look freshly fucked?"

She barks out a laugh. "No, I guess not. But that doesn't mean *something* didn't go down. You know…like you."

I throw a coaster at her. "Gross. Nothing happened."

"Uh-huh. Sure. Whatever you say."

"Anyway," I say loudly, "did Simon say why Winston called in?"

Wren shakes her head. "Nope."

"Huh." I shrug. "Well, whatever. It's not like him missing work is anything unusual. That boy never shows up to work."

"Actually…" Wren draws out. "This is the first time he's missed work in like a month."

"Is it really?"

"Yep," she replies. "I was shocked by it too, but my dad confirmed it this morning when we were going over payroll." She leans across the counter conspiratorially. "Between you and me, he even has some overtime in the books."

"No shit?"

She nods. "All the shit."

"I'm shocked," I say, twisting my mouth up. "I don't think I've ever known Winston to be so…responsible."

I don't know why, but there's this tiny ball of hope forming in my mind.

Maybe Winston's finally growing up, finding his drive.

For his sake, I hope so. He can't keep skulking around just waiting for everything to fall into place the rest of his life.

Granted, he doesn't have as much to worry about in comparison to the rest of the working class, but surely he doesn't expect to sit around doing nothing forever with no plans of growing up.

Perhaps he's finally realizing that too.

"Maybe you're the one rubbing off on him." She winks, and I know exactly what kind of rubbing off her mind is drifting toward.

I ignore her and pour myself a water.

"Did Porter get in touch with Doris?" I ask, shifting the subject away from anything to do with me and Winston because the last thing I want to think about is us in any sort of sexual situation.

"I'm not sure. They aren't moving here until next summer, so he's not in any rush. He's using the month he's here to do some house hunting."

"He has an entire *month* off work?" I whistle, taking a sip of my water. "Damn. Someone's fancy."

Wren laughs. "You're telling me. They were only coming to visit and then, two days into the trip, he decided he wants to move here, so he took a month away from the office."

"Seriously? Must be nice to just pack up and do what you want like that."

"Right? Foster was telling me he's pretty loaded. He owns an internet security company or something like that and is always traveling for it. I'm surprised he decided to buy out here since the home base for his business is in California." She steals my cup from my hand and downs half its contents. "Foster said he's divorced and still dealing with the fallout between him and his ex-wife. I guess maybe he's doing it to get away from her and get a fresh start? I don't know. Not my business. I just know Foster is happy to have him here."

"How old is his daughter?"

"Kyrie? She's six, and a total spitfire. Keeps Porter on his toes for sure."

"I can't wait for Riker to start talking. Right now, all he does is cry. And poop. Then cry some more. I'd just like for him to know any form of communication other than crying to get what he wants. It's tiring."

Her lips pull down because she knows I've been working myself into the ground since I found out I was pregnant.

Hell, I hardly took any time off when Riker was born. I couldn't afford to; I had bills to pay.

"How have you been sleeping at Winston's?"

"Like usual. I—"

No. That's not true.

Since I've been staying with her brother, I've had more nights of peaceful sleep than not, a miracle when you have a three-month-old.

"Actually," I say, "I've been sleeping pretty well. Sully's been a big help."

"Sully has? Really?"

I nod. "He's been watching Riker for me lately. The kid loves him, it keeps me from having to ask Winston to drive to Doris a million times a day, and it gives Sully something to do, so it works out for everyone."

"Except Doris," Wren points out.

"Well, not really. Now she's free to help Porter when he moves here, and I'm certain he'll pay her a hell of a lot more than I ever could, especially if he's looking for a live-in nanny."

"Fair point." She pushes off the stool she's been occupying. "We better get to work before my dad comes out and scolds us for not slaving away."

"Simon would never."

"Simon definitely would," says the man himself, coming through the back hallway. "He knows you have a lot of work to do before the lunch rush, so you better get your asses in gear."

"Dad, don't refer to yourself in third person. That went out of style in the nineties."

"To be fair, I don't think referring to yourself in the third person was ever cool," I point out.

"Yeah, what Drew said," Wren tells her father.

"How about you do what *Simon says* and get your rears to work."

"You're so bossy," his daughter grumbles.

"Well, I *am* the boss," he calls after her, feeling damn proud of his back-to-back dad jokes. He turns to me. "I was going to warn you to never have children, but that ship has clearly sailed."

I laugh. "You can say that again."

"I was going to warn you—"

I sigh. "If this is your ploy to get me to go work, you're succeeding."

He grins. "Good, but before you scamper off, how's your car coming along?"

"You know, you're the second person to ask about that today. I have no clue. I'd have to ask your son. He seems to have taken over all care for it."

"Huh." Simon grunts, hands going to his hips. "He keeps surprising me lately. Almost reminds me of the Winston before the accident, back when he had dreams and aspirations."

"What happened to him?"

"Honestly? I'm not sure. He just sort of…gave up. I tried telling him he was too young to be so old, but he doesn't seem to care."

"Did he do any therapy after the accident?"

"Sure. He had lots of physical therapy."

"No, I meant like"—I tap the side of my head—"that kind of therapy."

Simon shakes his head, frowning. "No. I think he uses his camera and the weed for that." He laughs when my brows shoot up. "Yes, Drew, I'm aware my son is a stoner. He probably gets that from me."

"You telling me you were a stoner? Being a teen in the seventies?" I gasp mockingly. "Oh, Simon, say it ain't so!"

"How dare you bring up my old age."

"Pfft. Old or not, I wouldn't kick you outta bed." I wink.

He laughs at me, shaking his head. "Get to work before I put you on dishes."

"One step closer to kitchen duty!" I call after him.

I push open the front door, relieved to finally be home.

Resting my back against the door, I take my first real breath in hours.

Simon wasn't kidding about us needing to get ready for the lunch rush. It was intense. We got hit with not one, but *two* after-soccer celebrations and were all running around ragged.

When we were still slammed for dinner, I called Sully to ask if it was okay to stay for a second shift to help Simon out.

Okay, okay—it was also to help out my barely-in-the-black checking account.

He agreed, and so I stayed, busting my ass all through the dinner rush and close.

It was all worth it though. Just thinking of the huge stack of bills in my apron makes my feet hurt just a little less.

"I thought we talked about you riding the bus so late at night."

My eyes shoot across the room, surprised to find Winston sitting on the couch.

There's no TV on, no laptop across his legs, no book in his hands.

He's just sitting there.

Waiting.

Though I'm not surprised.

When I left work tonight, Leroy, the only cabbie in town, was waiting to give me a ride home.

"You Drew Woods?" he asked, resting against his yellow clunker.

"Yes? Can I help you?"

"I was sent by that Daniels kid to give you a ride home. He already paid, now I just gotta deliver."

Of course Winston would send a cab. Heaven forbid I take the city bus home. It's beneath him for some reason.

Annoyed, I roll my eyes.

Screw him. I'm not here for his handouts. I can take care of myself.

"You said he paid already?"

"Yes, ma'am," Leroy says. "Tipped and everything."

"Well then you won't be mad if I decline the ride, will ya?"

"With the cash he gave me? Nah, kid. You do what you gotta do."

So I walked my happy ass to the bus stop and waited for twenty minutes for the next one to arrive.

"You talked about it." I push off the door, kicking my shoes away. "I pretended to listen. I don't understand why riding the bus is like a sin in your eyes."

"It's dangerous."

"I survived."

"Yeah, well, you might not have. People are creepy as fuck these days. Something could have happened to you. Then where would Riker be?"

I glare at him. "Don't you dare throw my son's wellbeing in my face like you have any say in how I run my life. If I didn't think I'd be safe, I wouldn't have done it. Besides, it's a tiny town. The only crime that happens here is a bike getting stolen by school bullies every now and then. I'm a big girl, Winston. I can handle myself."

"We have drifters."

"I truly feel like you're just grasping at straws right now because you're trying to make me feel bad about not calling and begging you for a ride like some damsel in distress." I pull the cash from my apron before I hang it on the hook near the door. "Check your ego before you really piss me off."

He rises from the couch. "It's not my ego I'm worried about. It's you."

"I stand by what I said. I can handle myself."

I hustle past him, heading for the bedroom.

"Do you really expect me to believe that's true? You can't even pay a fucking electric bill on time."

His words stop me in my tracks, and my eyes sting with embarrassment.

I march across the room toward him, fists balled at my sides, nails digging into my palms, my hand itching to make contact with his face.

"I hate you, Winston," I grind out. "I fucking *hate* you. Every single time I think you're not a complete prick, you prove me wrong. So fuck you. Fuck you, fuck you, fuck you. If you were that worried about me, maybe you should have been there for me today."

"I had shit to do."

"Oh? Like what? Bail on your family…*again*? You know Wren came in and covered your shift, right? She put *her* business on hold because you can't be bothered to show up for a shift at a fucking pizzeria and you want *me* to sit around waiting for you? To rely on you for rides to work?" I laugh. "Hilarious! You're the most unreliable person I know."

He grits his teeth together. "You don't know what you're talking about."

"I don't? So then you didn't call into work today to run off doing god knows what?"

"It was important," he argues. "But never mind all that. That's not what we're talking about here. We're talking about—"

"How I'm supposed to wait around on you to save me. Yeah, I

got that, but I'm telling you I can't depend on you for anything because you've proven time and time again that you're not that type of person. You only care about you."

"Let me get this straight: because I don't always show up to work at a—what was it again? Oh yeah, a *fucking pizzeria*," he mocks in the same tone I used, "I'm a complete shitbag? That job doesn't mean shit to me, Drew."

"That's just it, Winston!" I throw my hands into the air, adrenaline pumping through my veins. "Nothing means anything to you! You're on the back half of your twenties and have zero drive to do anything! How do you not see the problem with that?"

"I have drive," he argues.

"You sure as shit don't show it."

"You think just because I don't walk around telling every single person I meet about every little goddamn thing I do I don't have drive? Don't aspire to anything? That's bullshit. I aspire to plenty."

"Then why don't you act on any of it? Why don't you make something of all that talent you have? I know you do photography. I've seen you with the camera, and you clearly love being behind it. Why aren't you running a business with that? Why are you just working in your father's pizzeria making everyone else's life miserable?"

"Because…I…shit! Fuck!" He grabs at his hair. "I don't know, okay? I don't fucking know. I'm scared if I do something with my photography then that means I can't enjoy it anymore, means I can't just do it because I *want* to do it but because I then suddenly *have* to do it. I don't want the pressure."

I wave my hand around the house. "It's not like you have anything to worry about if you don't make it big. You're set for life."

He scoffs. "You have no idea what it feels like to have all this."

"Uh, what? Freeing? Yeah, Winston, must be *really* hard to have a fucking roof over your head. Must be really goddamn hard to not have to worry about that at all."

He gnashes his teeth. "You don't get it."

"Then explain it to me!"

"No!" he screams. "No! You clearly already have this idea of me in your mind painted nice and vibrant. What the fuck is the point?"

"I—"

I shake my head, my adrenaline losing steam fast, the exhaustion from the day and this pointless argument seeping in.

"I quit," I say. "This argument, trying to understand you—all of it. I just quit. Tomorrow, Riker and I are going back to my apartment. I made enough cash today to cover what I owe the electric company. I'll figure the rest out whenever."

"You can't leave. Your car isn't ready yet."

"I don't care. I'll take the bus you love so much."

I turn on my heel, heading for the bedroom. I'll be damned if I waste one more minute arguing with Winston and not sleeping in his insanely comfortable bed while I still can.

"Drew, wait."

"Good night, Winston."

I push the door open and stop in my tracks.

The first thing I notice is the music.

It's soft and low, but it's no lullaby.

It's Slayer, and it's playing from a lighted mobile swinging above a brand-new crib tucked into the corner of Winston's bedroom.

"What the…"

I walk closer, running my hand around the dark wood, admiring the curves and cuts. It's gorgeous. Exactly what I would have picked out.

There in the center, all swaddled up and snoring lightly, is Riker.

"Where did this come from?"

"This is what I had to do today." Winston's beside me, standing so close I can feel the heat radiating off his body. "This is why I missed work."

"You…you got this for me?"

"Well, for Riker. I think you're a bit too big for it." He grins. "I just felt bad for him because he was sleeping in a drawer. Besides, this is something he can have for a while. It converts into a bed for when he gets older."

"Winston…" It comes out as a whisper. "I…"

"Look."

My eyes follow his hand as he reaches up to the mobile.

It's not your typical farm or zoo animals hanging from strings.

No, this mobile is handmade.

And it's made up of pictures of me and Riker…pictures I didn't know were being taken. Us sleeping on the couch. Laughing on the back patio. Me feeding him, both of us half asleep. There's even one of him crying and me covered in vomit.

I laugh. "Winston, these are—"

"I hope you don't mind that I took the photos. It's just when my mom died, I realized we didn't have many pictures of her with us kids since she was always the one taking them. You don't even have anyone to take them for you, to give you that option. So, I took the liberty of snapping a few candid ones."

"Mind? Skulking around and taking photos of me and my baby is the sweetest, creepiest thing anyone has ever done for me."

He chuckles. "I thought so too."

I look up at him. "Thank you for this, Winston. I can't even tell you what it means to me. I…I'm sorry I was a bitch about you missing work today."

His thumb brushes over my cheek, wiping away the tears I didn't realize I was shedding.

I turn my head into his palm as he cups my cheek, loving the warmth of his rough hand.

"Don't apologize to me, Drew. Never apologize to me."

"I'm sorry."

He laughs.

"Sorry," I say again, realizing I just apologized for apologizing for apologizing.

"You're so annoying," he whispers teasingly.

"I think you secretly like it. And me."

He smiles, and my eyes drop to his full lips. "Sometimes."

"I think it's more than sometimes. You push my buttons an awful lot…almost like you like me."

He yanks me closer to him, our bodies flush against each other.

I groan at the contact. Not because it's Winston, but because it's been way too long since I've felt the touch of someone else.

Felt so…alive.

Our breaths are coming sharp, like we're chasing something.

And maybe we are.

Each other.

"I don't like you, Drew." I watch his lips move, mouth dangerously close to mine. "I hate you."

"I hate you too."

And then his lips are on mine.

Slice Eight

WINSTON

For the first time in longer than I can remember, I'm not high and can feel something other than constant pain.

Not just in my dick, either.

Drew's lips move beneath mine and I feel a moan hum through her before I hear it.

My hands tighten on her waist, and if I could pull her closer, I would.

But we're already flush against one another and she's writhing and rubbing against me like she hasn't felt anything like this before.

I haven't either.

Her hands inch up my chest, higher and higher until her fingers are curling into my hair. She pulls at the ends roughly, and now *I'm* the one moaning.

I grind my hips against her and trail my fingers over the exposed skin between her shirt and jeans, loving how soft she feels under my touch.

"You feel so soft," I mutter between kisses. "And you taste like wintergreen gum."

"Winston?"

"Yeah?"

"Shut the fuck up and keep kissing me."

Laughing, I press my mouth to hers again.

She pushes against me, trying to find a way to get some relief for what's building inside of her.

I feel it too.

Drew pulls at my shirt and I help her out, yanking the material over my head then bringing my lips back to hers.

Her eyes rake over me as she takes me in. I'm no stranger to stares from girls. I work fucking hard for the body I have.

But Drew's gaze feels like it's on a whole different level.

Her fingers crawl over the scar on my right shoulder where they had to surgically repair my rotator cuff.

The mark is thick, long. Ugly.

She grins up at me. "Is it weird that this kind of turns me on?"

I laugh, capturing her mouth as her hands roam over my chest, mapping every dip and ridge like she's trying to memorize them. Down, down, down until her fingers reach the waistband of my jeans.

She plays with the edge, dragging her nails over my skin with just enough pressure that it's making my cock throb.

Unsnapping the button with a flick of her wrist, she delves her hand inside, rubbing me over my boxer briefs.

"Fuuuuck." I hiss at the touch.

She grips me tighter, and I grit my teeth, embarrassingly close to ruining this before it even really starts because it's been too long since I've had a proper fuck.

I grab her hand. "Let's slow down a minute."

"I don't want to slow down. I want to do this. I need this."

This.

Not me.

Drew needs *this.*

Her words make me pause.

"What? What's wrong?" she asks, pushing her body into mine. "Don't stop now."

I set my hands on her shoulders, holding her away. "Stop."

"What is it?" She stares up at me with round, confused eyes. "Do you not want me?"

I laugh at her question, because it couldn't be further from the truth.

Do I want her? Hell yes.

But does she want me?

No.

"Of course I want you, Drew. But you don't want me."

Her brows crumple together. "I just said I want this. If you're worried about consent, you have it."

"Are you not listening to yourself? You want *this*, not *me*. Let that sink in before we take this any further. Will you wake up tomorrow regretting this? Will you be able to look me in the eye after I make you scream my name? Will you be okay with this?"

I place my lips against hers and she opens for me almost instantly. I sweep my tongue into her mouth, taking my time savoring her because I'm almost certain this will be the last time I'll get the chance tonight.

I pull away, ignoring the whimper that falls from her lips, trailing kisses up her cheek.

"If you aren't one hundred percent sure you want to do this with *me* and not just because your body is craving a certain touch, walk away now." I flick my tongue out, tasting the sensitive skin just below her ear. "Because if we do this, Drew, there's no turning back, no pretending it didn't happen."

I pull away from her entirely, watching as her knees shake without me holding her up. Her chest rises and falls rapidly as she gulps air in.

She blinks once. Twice.

I watch as the realization of what we're doing—or what we were almost doing—starts to fall into place.

I'm right.

Drew doesn't want me. She just wants to be touched.

No matter how badly I want to touch her, I am a greedy man and know if I start, I'll never want to stop.

And she's not ready for that.

I'm putting an end to this for her, because I sure as shit ain't doing it for me.

"I-I-I…" She clears her throat, lifting her chin. "You're right. I think this would have been a mistake."

"It would have been." *For you.*

We don't say anything for a long time. Just stand here, staring. Trying to gather the courage to leave the other.

It's harder than I thought it would be to walk away.

"We, uh, should probably go to bed."

I blow out a breath, nodding. "We should."

"I…I'm gonna take a shower, if that's okay?"

"Yeah. Of course. I'll, just…um, I'll go in after you."

She nods, moving toward the bathroom. The door clicks shut, and the sound is so loud. So final.

The water is turned on almost instantly, and I exhale for what feels like the first time tonight.

I toss myself onto the bed, scrubbing my hands over my face, trying to figure out what just happened.

What the fuck is wrong with me? I just stopped a beautiful girl from having sex with me. Since when do I do shit like that? When did I start taking the high road? Have I gone completely fucking insane?

Okay, maybe not *insane*.

I don't just like Drew.

I care about her, and not just a "It would really suck if you got hit by a car" kind of caring.

The real kind. The kind where I give a shit if she's happy or sad or mad. The kind where I *want* to know her problems and ambitions and her past…want to know her.

And that's my hang-up.

A fun fuck isn't in the cards for us because I won't be satisfied with just one night of moans and groans.

I'll want tomorrow too. And the next day. Hell, even the one after that.

I want Drew. For good.

The bathroom door swings open and I sit up, watching the steam filter through the doorway around Drew's figure.

My eyes travel up her legs—the very ones that could be wrapped around me right now if I hadn't let stupid fucking feelings get in the way and mess shit up. The shorts she has on are so tiny I can barely see them poking out under the hem of the t-shirt she's wearing…the one that's clinging to her still-damp body so tightly it tells me she's not wearing a bra. I can see her nipples protruding through the material.

She tucks her lip between her teeth, rubbing her legs together like it's more than just my eyes trailing along her skin right now.

I wish it was more than just my eyes. So does my hard cock.

But…she's not ready.

I push up from the bed, sliding past her and into the bathroom.

I slam the door closed, lean against it, and lock it. Not waiting another moment, I yank my jeans down and fist my cock.

"Fuck," I mutter, because it doesn't feel as good as Drew's hand felt on me, but it'll have to do.

I stroke myself hard. Fast. Unbridled.

There's a thump on the door. Then I hear it.

Soft whimpers and the unmistakable sound of fingers moving through wetness.

Drew's standing on the other side of the door.

Touching herself.

I squeeze my eyes shut, conjuring up what she must look like right now.

Back resting against the grain. Legs spread wide. Panties and shorts pulled to the side, too impatient to even take them off. Fingers flying over her clit as she chases the high.

I can hear her panting and the sound has me bucking my hips into my fist, stroking myself faster.

Tighter.

"Holy shit."

I grunt, so close to release.

Cupping my balls, I pull on them to try to stave off my orgasm; I don't want to finish alone.

I can still hear Drew rubbing herself, can still hear the sounds she's making, her moans growing brasher.

She's getting close too.

"Winston…"

It's distinctive, my name leaving her lips.

I come apart, ropes of cum splattering into my hand, nearly spilling out the sides with how much there is.

It's all because of Drew.

Gasping for air, I rest my head against the door, trying to get my legs to stop feeling like jelly and my heart rate to even out so I don't collapse on my way to the shower.

Drew expels a heavy breath and pushes off the door, and I take it as my cue to finally move before she realizes the water isn't running and we just got off together.

I crank the water to the highest heat I can get and kick my jeans off the rest of the way before diving under the steady stream.

I make quick work of scrubbing myself down and am stepping out of the shower within five minutes.

I towel off then wrap it around myself, slipping back into the bedroom.

Drew's on the bed now, the blanket tucked up around her, all the way to her chin.

I want so badly to crawl into the bed behind her and wrap my arm around her.

Not to do anything sexual—though I wouldn't be opposed—but just to lie next to her. To feel her body plastered against mine.

To be close to her.

Instead, I turn toward my dresser and pull out a pair of gym shorts, sliding them on under my towel, then toss it into the hamper in the corner of the room.

"Did you just skip undies?"

I glance over at her, smirking. "Were you just watching me change?"

She shrugs. "I was hoping you'd drop the towel."

I laugh. "Someone's still horny."

"Well, if *someone* hadn't turned me down, that wouldn't be an issue."

I open my mouth, but she cuts me off.

"I like that you were all chivalrous though. And thinking rationally, unlike me. Us sleeping together would have been a horrible idea, so I'm not mad."

It wouldn't have been that bad of an idea, I want to say.

But I don't.

Snapping my mouth closed, I give her a half smile. "Shouldn't you be sleeping?"

"I've been trying but I can't."

"Well, you should try harder. Your gremlin will probably be up in a few hours for a feeding."

Groaning, she rolls onto her back. "Don't remind me of how little sleep I get, Winston. The bags under my eyes mean I am well aware."

"I don't mind your baggy eyes."

She grins. "Thanks."

I start for the living room, knowing I need to try to get some sleep myself if I want to get up for a sunrise walk on the beach.

"Where are you going?"

I point toward the other room. "Couch."

"Don't be stupid. Get in here."

She doesn't have to ask me twice.

I round the bed and crawl into the other side, making sure there's still about a foot of distance between us. I'd rather not accidentally poke her with my morning wood.

Drew faces me, her eyes boring into mine.

"What?"

She shakes her head. "Nothing."

"Nothing is never nothing," I remind her.

"I-I th-th…"

Her voice breaks and a single tear rolls down her cheek. I don't even think twice before reaching over and wiping it away.

"Quit fucking crying," I say, but there's no malice in my words. "You know I hate that shit."

She chuckles, sniffling. "I know, I'm sorry. It's just…the crib. You have no idea how much it means to me, Winston."

"It's not a big deal, Drew. Certainly not anything to cry over."

"That's where you're wrong. It's a big deal to me. It's a big deal to Riker."

"Riker doesn't even realize he's not sleeping in a drawer."

"Babies are smarter than you think," she contends as I reluctantly drop my hand from her face, resting it between us. "I'm being serious here, Win. I didn't have much growing up. I didn't live a life of luxury. There were a lot of times where I only had peanut butter sandwiches for weeks at a time. I didn't know my father, and my mother wasn't exactly compassionate." Her fingertips run over my open palm, tracing the lines on my hand. "I want to give Riker a better life than I had. I want him to know he's loved. That crib…it's proof. So, yeah, it does mean something to him, or at least it will when I tell him the story of it and how his best friend Winston got it for him."

Anger floods through me. It's a familiar feeling for me, but it's not me I'm angry for.

It's Drew.

Everybody deserves to know what it feels like to be loved.

Especially her.

"Sully is going to be pretty bummed that I'm Riker's best friend and not him."

She laughs. "I won't tell if you don't."

"Deal."

Her fingers lace with mine and I rub my thumb over the back of her hand. Her eyes trace my movements, and a small smile forms on her lips.

She moves her dark eyes to mine. "Thank you. Seriously."

"You're welcome. Seriously. Now go to sleep."

"Good night, Winston."

"Night, Drew."

Slice Nine

DREW

"Son of a bitch!"

"Now, now, that's no way to address your child."

I glower back at Winston, who's leaning against the doorframe of his bedroom. "Go away, Winston."

"Haven't we established by now that this is *my* house? I can be in any room I want at any time I want to be in it."

"I pray you walk in next time I'm taking a shit."

The corners of his lips twitch, but other than that, he shows no reaction to my words.

"Why all the cursing? You've been annoying me for the last two minutes with your stomping around and hollering. Two minutes is too long, especially when it comes to you."

"Is that a line the ladies feed you often?" I smirk, and his eyes narrow. "I'm just having issues staying organized in here without some of my essentials. I'm used to a particular system at home, and being here is throwing off my entire routine. I'm tired of living out of a damn bag, and you didn't pack any good clothes for me. I look like a street rat whenever I'm not in uniform."

"To be fair, you look like a street rat when you *are* in uniform too."

I flip him the middle finger, and he pretends to catch it, shoving it into his back pocket.

"I'll keep that promise for later."

I disregard him and continue trying to sort through the mess that's taking up most of Winston's bed.

"I have an idea."

I peek up at him again. "Oh. I didn't realize you were still here."

He shoves off the doorjamb. "What if you just moved in here?"

I blink at him.

Then fall into a fit of laughter because he can't be serious.

"What's so fucking funny?" he barks, brows slammed down, arms crossed over his chest.

Are his arms always that big? Does he always look that good in deep red?

"Your joke," I say, pushing away the stupid thought. "That's what's funny. I can't live here. Not with you."

"Why not?"

"Because I have a baby."

"You do? No way! Is that what I found sleeping in my dresser drawer?"

"Hardy-har," I mock. "I'm being serious, Winston."

"I'm being serious too, Drew. Just move in here with me."

I watch him closely, waiting for the punchline, waiting to see how he's going to rip the rug out from under my feet.

The punchline never comes.

He never rips the rug.

Winston is being one hundred percent serious right now.

"Why?"

"Why what?"

"Why would you want us to move in with you?"

"Because you need a safe place to live. Riker needs you to have a safe place to live. You need heat, water, food—the essentials. Need someone with a reliable car to get you around when yours inevitably goes caput. You need stability. I can offer you all of that."

I open my mouth to argue with him, but he holds his hand up, stopping every excuse I have at the ready from tumbling out of my mouth.

"Don't argue. Just think about it. It's a serious offer. You and Riker can stay here as long as you need to until you get back on your feet. Move all your stuff in here. It's not a massive house or anything, but we can make it work for the time being. Besides, this car repair will most likely cost a pretty penny, and going back to your apartment and saddling yourself with all those bills and rent is just going to set you further and further behind." He lifts a shoulder and backs out of the room, still staring at me. "Keep that in mind while you're thinking about it."

He disappears, leaving me standing here with a million questions and just as many reasons why this could never work running through my head.

I can't live with Winston.

I hate him too much to live with him.

We'd do nothing but fight all the time. He'd drive me crazy and I'd try to kill him.

There is no possible way this could work.

Unless we just kissed all the time, because I don't seem to mind him then.

No!

I am *not* thinking about it. I *can't* think about it.

I've spent too much time over the last two days thinking about kissing him again. I can't waste another second doing it.

With those thoughts off the table, I still can't find a good reason for us to live together.

Well, besides all the ones he listed…the very compelling ones.

I start adding up my bills in my head. Then I tack on how much I'm ballparking the car repairs will cost.

I tally up all the diapers I'm going to need, the formula vouchers don't cover, and basics just to get by.

At the rate I'm going, it looks like I'll be broke forever.

Shit.

I think Winston's right. I think it *would* be a good idea if Riker and I moved in here.

I'd feel awful putting him out like this, but he *did* offer, and it *was* genuine.

Before I can talk myself out of it, I march toward the living room, ready to tell him yes.

Only my feet screech to a halt when my eyes land on the scene on the back patio.

Winston's standing out there, one of those dreadful cigarettes in hand. Smoke is billowing around him, and although I think smoking is disgusting, I'd be lying if I said he's ever looked sexier than he does in this moment.

His shirt is stretched over his broad, muscled shoulders. His jeans hang low on his hips, hugging his ass just right.

How is it possible he's so attractive *and* so annoying?

As if he can feel my eyes on him, he peers at me over his shoulder. Slowly, he turns, resting his back against the rail. He brings the cigarette to his mouth, the end turning a bright orange as he takes a long drag. My teeth sink into my bottom lip. I've never been so jealous of a cigarette in my entire life.

A new cloud of smoke forms around him, swirling with the old as he slowly releases it through his lips.

God, I feel like a fool watching him smoke and getting so turned on by it.

His mouth turns up in the corners, like he knows he's affecting me.

Like he's teasing me on purpose.

Stupid, sexy jerk.

I force myself out of the haze and march toward him, sliding open the glass door and stepping out into the cool night air.

"Did you think about my offer?" he says coolly.

"I have conditions."

"Of course you do." He shakes his head, coughing out a laugh and stubbing his cigarette out in the ashtray. "Let's hear them."

"What happened between us the other night, it—"

"Our kiss," he says, as if either of us need a reminder of what I'm talking about. "Go on."

"Yes, that—it can't happen again. It *won't* happen again. Just because I'll be living here does not mean it's pussy galore all the time."

He barks out a laugh. "Pussy galore, huh?"

"Yep." I wave a hand over my lady bits. "This is a no-go zone for you."

"So we can still make out?"

"No!" I stomp my foot like a child. "No touching. This is strictly platonic."

"We can't fuck as friends then? Well, hell. There go all the plans I had to bend you over the kitchen table during breakfast while Sully watched."

"Winston…" I drop my head into my hand, already exhausted

from talking to him for the short time I've been out here.

"I'm kidding, Drew. I don't expect you to blow me every night for room and board. All I ask is that you pick up after yourself and Riker and we're square."

"Square? You can't let me stay here for free and not do anything. That's not how I work."

"Well that's how I work."

"It is not. You're just trying to do me a favor, is all. You just feel bad for me."

"Not true. Sully doesn't pay any rent and he definitely doesn't blow me. He stays for free, too."

"He doesn't pay for *anything*?"

He grunts. "I didn't say that."

"Then let me pay for something too."

"With what money, Drew? Besides, isn't the whole point of you staying here to save money? That sounds counterproductive to me."

Shit. He has a point there.

"Then can I at least cook for you guys? I have some mean skills in the kitchen."

"Kitchen skills but no bedroom skills—noted."

I huff. "I'm going to assume that's a deal then."

"It's a deal. Do you want to go get your stuff?"

"Like…now?"

"No, I was thinking six months from now, maybe on the third Tuesday in February. Yes, now."

"Oh," I say quietly. "Okay. I guess we can do it now. Let me just go get ready and see if Sully can handle Riker for a bit."

"It shouldn't take long. You don't have much of anything."

I want to be offended by his comment about my meager possessions, but it's too accurate for me to be mad about.

"Be ready in five," he says, brushing past me, making sure to rub against me as he goes back into the house.

It's a simple touch, really, but it still feels so good to have him against me again, no matter how fleeting it is.

What the hell did I just agree to?

Winston wasn't kidding. I don't have much at all.

In fact, it's so minimal it only takes a single truckload.

Sully was cool about watching Riker and even offered up his truck so we could grab everything in one go.

Not like there's much to pile into the bed.

Hell, we even have some spare room.

All my clothes can fit into a large box and Riker's in a small one. I only ever kept enough dishes for two people, so there isn't much to pack in the kitchen either.

The biggest pieces we're taking away are my broken entertainment center, my old dresser, and the lumpy couch I've slept on for months now.

I sold everything else when I found out I was pregnant and squirreled away the cash.

"You can call your landlord tomorrow and get everything sorted with him, right?" he asks when we pile back into the truck after everything's loaded.

"Sure," I tell him, though I have zero intentions of doing so.

Call me crazy, but I don't plan to walk away from the month-to-month lease I have with my landlord—if you can even call the guy that—until I know things will pan out and Riker and I truly do have a place to stay at Winston's.

I'm not about to count my chickens before they hatch.

Besides, my rent is dirt cheap at this place. It's how I'm able to afford to keep living there. Luckily, if I'm not spending the gas money going back and forth to work, I can save that in case I need rent again next month.

We ride in silence for a few miles, Winston the first one to break it.

"You know, when I first met you, I didn't expect you to live in the kind of apartment you do. I didn't expect you to be so…frugal."

"You mean deadass broke? Barely scraping by?"

He grimaces at my bluntness. "Yes."

"I wasn't always so bad off. That came with being dumped by my baby's father."

"Fucking douchebag," Winston seethes.

I laugh. "Amen to that."

He shifts gears when we pull away from the stoplight, and I watch as the muscles in his arms jump.

Stop it.

I can*not* be checking him out if we're going to be living together now.

It's just not going to be a thing.

It can't be.

"You're a really good mom, Drew."

His out-of-the-blue compliment has me whipping my head in his direction.

"What?"

"I said you're a really good mom. You're doing a good job providing for your son. He's going to appreciate it so much when he's older and understands the sacrifices you're making. I'll make sure of it."

Tears prick my eyes, but I blink them away.

Clearing my throat, I say, "Thank you. Not just for that, but for everything. It means a lot."

He nods but doesn't say anything else.

And we spend the rest of the trip in silence.

Slice Ten

WINSTON

"When did you say Mr. Schwartz would be done with my car?"

"I didn't."

Drew lifts a brow at me. "Well, do you have any info? I can't be without a car forever. I can't keep depending on you to give me rides, you know."

This weird feeling settles in my gut as what she says truly sinks in.

She's right. She can't depend on me forever.

I have to keep reminding myself this isn't permanent. Drew living here is only temporary. Eventually she's going to leave. She has a life to live that doesn't include crashing at someone else's house, no matter how convenient it is.

Riker has a routine to get back to.

I have a life to get back to.

Not to mention the fact that we still don't get along.

We might be temporarily living together and sharing a bed at night, but we aren't suddenly best friends or anything. We're a hell of a lot more civil with one another, but things aren't magically perfect between us.

She still drives me wild, and not just in the *I want to take you to bed* kind of way.

She's messy. She's bossy. A total know-it-all. Always in my space and my business.

Despite all that, I'm not ready for her to leave yet. Which is why I haven't told her the car is ready. It's *been* ready…and paid for.

Telling her would light too much of a fire under her ass. She'd be bailing out of here at the first sign of things looking up, whether she's truly ready to or not. Then she'd just be back at square one and I'd have to rescue her.

Again.

Also, not that I'm willing to admit it out loud, I've grown used to having her around. This house is kind of lonely when she's not here.

Drew makes me laugh. Gives me someone to spar with. Keeps me on my toes twenty-four seven.

Besides, Riker and I are starting to bond. Ever since that night I bounced him back to sleep, he's taken to me.

Which is why he's chilling on the couch next to me watching *SpongeBob*—Sully swears it's his favorite—while Drew gets ready to take a shower.

"It's not done yet," I lie. "It'll probably be another week."

"Seriously?" she groans. "This is taking *forever*."

"Hey, he's doing it in his spare time, and for cheap. It'll be done when it's done. Besides, you have room and board and a ride in the meantime. It's not a big deal."

"I just hate being a leech."

"No, you're just stubborn and don't want to accept help."

"Exactly—being a leech."

"Two totally different things, but whatever," I say. "As soon as it's done, I'll let you know."

"Fine. I'm hitting the shower. Taking an extra-long one, by the way. Gonna enjoy this hot water while I have it."

She disappears into my bedroom, shutting herself into the bathroom.

"Your mother is crazy," I whisper to Riker. "Absolutely insane." He giggles. "But we like her anyway, huh?"

He giggles again, and the sound makes me smile.

I turn back to the TV, settling into the comfy couch I no longer have to sleep on.

Since Drew and I have been sharing a bed, it's the best streak of good sleep I've had in ages, which is surprising because I haven't taken a single hit of weed since I was a complete tool to her.

At first, it was because I was afraid of what my loose lips would let fly if I smoked again. I hadn't realized the fog I was living in, so wrapped up in the way the high chased the pain away. When I hurt Drew, when I said those awful things to her and saw the way they broke her, it made me realize maybe the weed was making me a different person, and it was a version of me I didn't like.

Weed affects people differently, and apparently it doesn't just make me lazy—it makes me an ass.

Then there's the kiss.

The one that made me soar.

It was better than any high marijuana can give me.

I haven't felt that good in a long fucking time, and I want to feel it again.

So I've been powering through, ignoring the growing throbs in my shoulder and back and riding the high of the memory of Drew's kiss—just the memory, because much to my chagrin, our lips haven't touched again.

It's not because I haven't wanted to or we haven't had the opportunity, but because I want to be sure Drew is kissing me because she wants to kiss *me* and not just *someone.*

I laugh at something Patrick says, and Riker giggles like he gets it too.

He's four months old now, and I swear he's getting bigger every time I look at him.

"Was that funny?" I ask, lifting him onto my lap so I can bounce him on my knee. "Did Patrick say something funny? Is he goofy? Is he—oh fuck. What the hell is that smell? Jesus fuck!"

I gag, and Riker laughs again.

"You little…" I push up off the couch, holding him away from me at arm's length, and grab the changing pad from the diaper bag.

I'm getting way too used to changing shitty diapers lately.

I get him situated on it, snap the tabs off, and peel back the loaded diaper like the fucking pro I am.

Only there's no shit.

He just farted *really* fucking bad.

I frown down at him. "You little fibber. You didn't shit." He laughs, and I tickle his belly. "You just have gas. What a little stinker. You—"

It hits me before I can react.

Riker pisses straight onto my face.

"WHAT THE FUCK!"

I place my hand over the stream, trying to block it as best I can.

I grab a wet wipe and clean my face off, grab a new diaper, and get him changed before he can piss on me some more.

He's happy as can be the entire time.

I stand him up and he gives me a shit-eating grin like he didn't just whiz all over me.

"You're a monster," I tell him.

He giggles, but then his laughter quickly subsides into tears, and he's having an all-out screaming fit.

I grab his binky and take him to the bedroom, turn on his mobile—the greatest thing I've ever created because he absolutely loves it—and place him in his crib.

He calms down within a minute.

"Good boy," I say, rubbing his head.

I march into the bathroom and yank the curtain open.

"Winston! What the fuck! I'm naked!"

She does a poor job of covering herself, but it wouldn't matter anyway. I don't even care about checking her out in this moment.

"Your son just pissed all over me."

"W-What?" she sputters then looks at my shirt, which is covered in pee.

She bursts into laughter, her hands slipping away from her tits, a nipple popping out of her attempt to cover herself.

Okay, *now* I'm checking her out.

"Stop it!" she says when she notices she's showing off more than she wanted, shielding herself once again.

"What?" I roll my eyes. "Nothing I haven't seen before."

"You haven't seen *me* naked before."

"Please. You see one naked chick, you've seen them all."

Except that's not true.

A naked Drew blows all the other naked girls out of the water.

But I won't give her the satisfaction of knowing that.

She stomps her foot, annoyed I'm not blown away by her

nakedness.

"Can I help you, Winston?"

"Yeah. You can save me some hot water." I reach in and cut the flow. "I need a shower. Because, you know, your kid just pissed on me."

She cranks the water again. "Not my fault you don't know how to change a diaper properly."

I reach for the handle once more but have a better idea.

"You know what? You're right. Why wait to shower when you're done? I'll just hop in with you now."

I yank my shirt over my head, tossing it to the side, and reach for the button on my jeans.

"Winston!"

I unzip them. "Scoot over, Drew."

"No! Oh my god. Get out!"

I shove the denim down my legs and step out of them. I hook my thumbs into my boxer briefs. "Last chance."

She doesn't budge, and I pull them down just an inch.

"Fine!" she concedes, scooting out of the stall. "It's all yours."

She moves quickly, snatching the towel off the hook and wrapping it around herself before I can get a good look at her.

"You're a jerk. I'm glad Riker peed on you."

"Your kid is a monster," I say, stepping into the shower, pulling the curtain closed, and stepping under the lukewarm water. "Son of a bitch. Dammit, Drew! You used all the hot water!" I call out.

From over top of the shower, I'm assaulted by towel after towel.

"What the…"

I glance down at the pile. Every single towel is now sitting in the bottom of the tub, completely soaked.

"You little…" I glower at her shadow through the curtain. "Now I see where your kid gets his mean streak from."

Drew flips me the bird and turns on her heel, leaving me stranded under the cold water and with no way to dry off.

And yet, I still don't hate her.

"Did you talk to your landlord?"

"Yep."

"Liar."

She turns toward me, wiping her hands on the front of her apron. "Excuse me?"

"You're a fucking liar. You didn't talk to him. You didn't break your lease."

Her eyes dart around the kitchen, looking anywhere but at me, really.

She's caught, and she knows it.

"How do you know that?"

"I went by today and grabbed your mail because it hasn't been forwarded here yet. Your landlord had no idea you had moved out."

"Why were you getting my mail?"

"I was in the area, so I figured I'd stop in and grab it for you."

"Geeze, you're turning into a big softy lately."

I ignore the barb. "Why didn't you break your lease?"

"Because this is only temporary, Winston. I'm not living here forever, just until I can pay off my car repairs and get my shit back together. This isn't real. That apartment is. I need to keep paying on it so I don't lose it."

"You already did."

Her face twists into an expression of anger.

"What the fuck did you do, Winston?" Her tone is low, almost scary. You know, minus her being well over six inches shorter than me and all.

"I took care of it for you."

"Please tell me you're joking."

"I'm not. He didn't charge that much, just half a month's worth of rent when I threatened to report his ass for all the mold I saw in my short time there. So you're square."

"I am *not* square!" She slams her hand down on the counter then points angrily at me. "You had no right to do that!"

"I did it because you're too fucking chicken to do it. Why can't you just accept that I'm trying to help you?"

"Why can't you just stop? I didn't ask for your help!"

"Well too fucking bad, because you got it."

Her stare is so hot, so full of fire.

But I'm not scared.

"By the way, your car is ready. And paid for."

I walk out of the kitchen, ignoring her screams.

I know she hates me just a little bit more now, but it was worth the risk.

Slice Eleven

DREW

Something's changed since we kissed and I moved in.

It's not just the fact that I can't stop thinking about the way Winston's lips felt on mine and that I'm now hornier than ever lying next to him in bed every night.

Or that I'm now completely stuck with him since he broke off my lease.

Or that I'm now indebted to him since he paid off my car repairs.

It's something else.

Something…more. Bigger.

My feelings toward him have turned from hate to…something else.

I don't necessarily like him, because he can't stop trying to rescue me.

But I don't *hate* him, and there's a good chance I might even be beginning to understand him. He's not as mean and vile as he pretends to be. He actually gives a shit about people.

He's just scared.

I don't know why he decided to take it upon himself to help me, but I won't let him get away with it. I'll repay him one day. I don't know how yet, but I will.

"How?"

"No wonder my dad won't let you into the kitchen. You can't even make the most basic meal ever."

I peel my attention from the platter I'm arranging and train it on Winston. I was so deep in my own head, I didn't even realize I spoke out loud.

"What are you jabbering about?"

"I asked you to start the mac and cheese and you just asked me how."

"Oh." I wipe my hands across my apron and cross the room. "I wasn't paying you any attention. Also"—I snatch the blue box from his hands—"I am *not* making that shit. I'll make it from scratch."

He scowls at me. "Hey! That was expensive."

"It was likely less than a dollar. You can afford it."

"What's wrong with the boxed stuff?"

"Everything."

"You telling me you've never eaten boxed mac and cheese before?"

"Of course I have," I say, sliding past him and to the pantry. "But I'm not feeling it today. I want to make something nice for our friends."

That and I love any excuse to create in the kitchen. I don't get to do it much with Simon kitchen-blocking me at work, so I'll take it where I can get it.

He sighs. "Remind me again why we're having a cookout?"

"We're having a baby shower."

"But you're not pregnant. Or is there something you need to share?"

I look at him pointedly, because the fucker knows I most definitely am not pregnant, then go back to rooting around for the ingredients for the mac and cheese. "It's a postnatal baby shower."

"Aren't baby showers supposed to happen *before* you have the baby?"

"Technically, yes, but that didn't happen."

"Because you're stubborn," he reminds me for the billionth time. "You didn't want anyone to buy you gifts because you didn't want to come off as 'needy' even though literally everyone has baby showers."

"You don't sound annoyed by this at all," I sass.

"You drive me crazy. You make everything ten times more complicated because you don't want to be complicated. You're the most counterproductive person ever."

"That's not true."

"You're literally making mac and cheese from scratch when there is a perfectly good box of it right here."

He shakes said box at me, and I snatch it from his hands, tossing it into the trash can.

"Drew!"

"What?" I say innocently. "It's garbage. I just put it where it belongs."

The doorbell chimes, and Winston starts for the door to let our guests in, shaking his head and muttering about how annoying I am.

"Annoying or not, we're about to have some bomb-ass mac and cheese!" I call after him.

He chuckles, and I grin, turning to the pantry.

"Something happened between you two, didn't it?"

Sully's sudden appearance startles me, and I drop the box of noodles I'm holding.

"Are you a fucking ninja or something?"

"Sorry." He gives me a small smile. "Didn't mean to startle you."

"For not meaning to, you did a damn good job."

"That doesn't answer my question." He crosses his arms over his chest. "Did something happen? You two seem more…snappy than usual, like you're trying to overcompensate for something. Is it because Winston butted his nose in where it doesn't belong like he always does, or is it something else?"

I pause, the box I just picked back up beginning to shake in my hand at the thought of admitting out loud that Winston and I kissed, that things aren't just peachy between us and there's this added layer of sexual tension.

Is it so palpable that Sully's now butting his nose into it?

Or is he just curious and trying to bait me into admitting it on my own?

"You don't have to tell me anything, Drew," Sully says softly. "But just in case you're wondering"—his eyes flit to the shaking box—"your silence is speaking volumes."

"It was a one-off thing," I confess. "It won't be happening again."

"What won't be happening again?" Wren asks, blazing into the kitchen like she owns the place. "What'd I miss?"

Sully waits for me to say something.

I don't.

He grins at my best friend. "Drew's making boxed mac and cheese to go with dinner."

I blow out a breath, relieved yet incredibly annoyed at the same time.

I despise boxed mac and cheese. It reminds me too much of the times in my life when I had no options for dinner except for the eighteen-cent rectangle of crap I had to survive off of for weeks at a time. It didn't matter how I dressed it up—hot sauce, barbeque, bologna chunks, stale breadcrumbs—it was still the same shit. Makes me want to vomit just thinking about it.

Besides, I know if I make it, Winston's going to be the victor of our tiff.

Fucking Sully.

Wren crinkles her nose. "Really? But your homemade mac and cheese is the best."

"I don't have a choice in the matter," I grind out, shooting daggers at Sully.

He just grins, slipping out of the room like he didn't just stir up a whole bunch of shit *and* find out some personal information about me all at once.

Wren rolls up her sleeves and runs her hands under the faucet. She then holds them up like the doctors on TV shows do after they've scrubbed in for surgery.

"I'm ready. Put me in, Coach."

"Actually," I say, looking around, "I'm pretty much all set for now. I just need to start the"—I gulp—"mac and cheese about eight minutes before the meat is done."

"Oh." She frowns, dropping her hands. "Where's Riker?"

"Napping. During his own party."

"The audacity!" She gasps, heading for the fridge. She pulls open the big silver doors and grabs two bottles. "Well, while he continues to be a little bum, let's crack open a beer and gab. I feel like I haven't seen you in ages."

She slides a drink my way, and I hesitate to grab it.

Not because I don't like beer, but because I'm a little afraid to drink with Winston around.

I don't trust myself around him.

Not after our kiss.

"Come on, live a little. Your kiddo is napping and there are plenty of people here to help watch him. It's been way too long since you've relaxed and let loose. At least have *one* beer with me."

I stare longingly at the booze, my nervous system already craving the cooldown it will provide.

She's right. I could use something to dull this constant edge I seem to be on.

"Fuck it." I grab the beer and crack it open, tipping the sweet liquid back and loving the way it slides down my throat.

"That's my girl!" She clinks her bottle against mine. "Cheers! Now tell me how it's going living with my brother. He seems grumpier than usual. Are you not putting out to pay for your stay here?"

The beer I just took a swig of goes flying from my mouth at her words.

"Wren Amanda Daniels!"

She wipes her face off. "First, that was disgusting. Second, what? What'd I say?"

"Me and Winston." I shudder. "It's gross."

"Fine." She rolls her eyes, leaning against the counter, peeling at the label on her bottle. "At least tell me you're sleeping with Sully."

"Does Foster not fuck you enough? Why do you seem extra horny today? That's usually my role in our friendship."

"Foster fucks me just fine." She shimmies her hips, waggling her brows. "I don't know what's up with me. I'm just feeling frisky lately, like everything Foster does turns me on. I think it's the whole upcoming nuptials thing. It's making me all hot and bothered knowing I'm finally going to be Mrs. Foster Marlett."

"Are you even allowed to say 'finally' when it comes to Foster? You spent years and years completely blind to the fact that the man is head over heels in love with you."

"Yeah, yeah," she grumbles. "Don't remind me of my

shortcomings. I am well aware of the years I spent away from him. We also got a fun reminder of it last week when we met with the financial adviser."

"Did it not go well?"

"I mean, it did. It was just an hour of us sitting there having to listen to how badly his ex-wife screwed up his credit. He's going to be repairing it for a while still. I had to co-sign on a few things for him, and I could tell it made him uncomfortable to have to depend on me."

"Well, he had better get used to it." I shrug. "Marriage is a partnership and sometimes you gotta lean on each other a little bit, especially when you don't want to."

Wren snorts. "You are *so* not the one to be giving out leaning advice. You've been complaining about Winston left and right when he's going out of his way to help you and Riker right now."

I frown. "I don't *mean* to complain. It's not that I'm not appreciative."

"I know that."

"It's just… Well, it's hard for me, ya know? I've been on my own for so damn long and I've always had to fend for myself. It's difficult for me to let anyone else in and help me out."

"I get it," she says. "I didn't want Foster to help me before either, but I'm glad he did. It made us stronger, in a way."

"How are you both so stubborn? Is that a twin thing?"

"I prefer the term strong-willed."

I grin. "I'll have to throw that one Winston's way next time he calls me stubborn."

"Now *that* I find hilarious." She grabs a carrot stick from the tray I have prepared, dunking it into the tub of ranch I set out. "Winston calling someone stubborn is like a trashman saying the trash doesn't stink. It just doesn't make any sense."

She pops the carrot in her mouth, crunching loudly.

"Okay, first, I don't think that's an actual saying. Second, what do you mean?"

"His recovery after the accident—he was *so* difficult. Didn't want to go to any doctor appointments, didn't want anyone's help. He refused therapy, ignored his prescriptions. Didn't want to do anything. We had to fight hard for him to actually finish physical therapy so he could use his arm full range. I think the only reason he did was to be able to use his camera again." She shakes her head. "It was a mess. *He* was a mess."

"I…I didn't know all that." I sip on my beer. "How did I not know all that?"

"We were new friends," she explains. "I didn't want you to have to witness all our family drama."

I bark out a laugh. "Oh, Wren. You have no idea what family drama really is. Trust me."

She shrugs, dipping more carrots into the ranch. "Good lord, these are good."

"They're just baby carrots. Calm down."

I spin toward the fridge, grabbing the bag of veggies to replenish what Wren has eaten already.

My mind is racing as little pieces of the Winston I know today begin to fall into place.

The way he groans whenever he stands. The slow gait he has when he has to walk upstairs. The disturbing pop I hear when he reaches up to the top shelf in the pantry.

I don't think Winston ever finished physical therapy properly. I think he lied, think he pushed through the pain and fed them all a bunch of bullshit so he didn't have to go anymore.

He's still living with the pain from the accident, and he's using weed to cope with it. He smokes to feel everything, because right now all that's inside of him is pain.

Which makes me feel like an ass, because I shamed him for it.

If there's one thing I hate more than admitting I'm wrong, it's admitting I'm wrong to *him*. He gloats too much, like he enjoys seeing me so off-kilter, and the thought of Winston reveling in my mortification drives me mad. But I owe him an apology.

Maybe I was wrong before. Maybe I don't like Winston.

Maybe I'm just going insane because he makes me that way.

Or maybe I'm just overthinking all of this because I feel indebted to him.

Yes. That's totally it. I'm confusing obligations with feelings.

I think…

"Wren, can I ask you something?" I dump more veggies into the tray around her quick fingers.

She pauses midbite. "This sounds serious."

"It's not," I promise. "It's kind of silly, actually."

"Shoot." She shoves the rest of the carrot into her mouth, leaning against the counter, ready to be my ear.

"How did you know you liked Foster?"

Her brows shoot up. "Okay, not gonna lie, that is so not what I was expecting you to ask."

"What were you thinking?"

"I honestly don't know, but it wasn't that."

"If it's dumb, just ignore me." I push away from the counter and return the veggies to the fridge. "I'm just having an off day. I think my hormones are still out of whack from the baby. I—"

"I don't mind answering," she cuts in. "It's just a hard question to answer because Foster and I have so much history between us."

"Well…can you try?"

She nods, lips pursed, trying to find the best way to describe it.

"See, when a man and a woman haven't had sex for a *long* time and they're super horny, they—"

"Wren!" I throw a dish towel at her. "I'm being serious right now!"

"I am too. At first, for me, it was about being horny and wanting to get back out into the dating world. Then you"—she looks at me pointedly—"had the fake dating idea and set things into motion for me and Foster. I truly didn't think of him as anything other than my good friend or my brother's best friend. He was just Foster. He wasn't anything special."

She grins to herself, and I love the way her face lights up when she talks about him.

I wonder if I'll ever have that same sort of feeling about anyone.

"Then something shifted. Spending time with him just felt so…right. Like that was where I was supposed to be, with him. It was subtle. It didn't happen overnight. It just happened."

"But how did you know you wanted to take it further with him? Like…you know…"

"How did I know I wanted to beat cheeks with him?"

I cringe. "Can you not?"

"Sorry." She laughs, sounding anything but. "It's just funny seeing *you* be shy about sex."

"I just don't want the guys to hear."

"Ah, yes, good point. They'll tease you mercilessly." She leans closer. "To answer your question, I didn't realize it *was* going to get sexual. He just kissed me one day, and after that, I couldn't think about anything else. He was seared into my head. My breath would come in short spurts just thinking about it. The kiss made me feel…"

"Alive?" I say.

That's how Winston made me feel.

Like I could breathe easy for the first time in a long damn time, even though he was stealing the breath from my lungs.

It was a weird sensation, but I want to feel it again so badly.

Kissing him again is all I can think about.

Maybe I'm *not* confusing my feelings at all…

"No." Wren breaks into my thoughts. "Horny. Like *super* horny. Like *I could jump his bones at any point in time* horny."

"That sounds…"

"Insane, right?" She nods. "He has a way of doing that too, making me feel crazy—but in a good way. Not one of those *look at me wrong and I'll bury you then help them look for you* kinds of crazy, but the okay kind."

"Okay." I push off the counter. "You scare me a bit, but I get it."

Winston makes me crazy too.

Sometimes I think it's in the bad way, but perhaps that's because I'm still figuring him out.

Maybe if I let him in a little, he'll let me in, and it won't be so scary anymore.

"So…I gotta ask," Wren starts as I untie my apron and set it on the counter. "Do you, uh, like someone I should know about?"

I gulp.

Wren is my best friend and I know for a fact she'd have no issues with the idea of me being into her brother. She's chill like that.

But I am by no means ready to tell her about it.

Not because I'm trying to hide anything from her, but because even *I* don't understand what's going on with us right now or how I'm really feeling toward him.

"N-No. It's not that," I lie. "I, um, was just curious, is all." I wave my hand. "Hormones."

"Right." She eyes me curiously. "Because if you *do* like someone, that's okay. I can put in a good word with them, if you'd like." She waggles her brows. "He might be new in town, so I don't know if he's looking, but based on how he was looking at you at Slice, I bet he's interested too."

My brows squish together.

Looking at me at Slice? Who was at Slice? Winston was there, but he was all kinds of pissy that day, so surely she doesn't mean him.

She has to mean…

"Porter?" I say. "Is that who you're thinking of?"

She grins. "He's so cute, isn't he?"

"No!" I rush out. "Well, I mean, yes. I have eyes and he's definitely hot, but it's not Porter. I don't like him."

"Oh." Her lips pull down. "I thought the single-parent thing was a total turn-on for you, given your situation and all."

Right. My situation.

The one I didn't even think about until just now because my baby is so ingrained in my soul I forget he's not everyone's cup of tea.

I can't like Winston.

Not only because he doesn't like me, but because he also doesn't like kids.

He's been very explicit about that in the past.

Riker and me? We're a package deal. While Winston's letting us stay with him for a while, it's not permanent by any means. What he's doing to help us is hugely different than actually raising a kid.

"Well, it's not him—not that I like *anyone*," I stress.

"Right," she says warily. "You were just curious."

"Right." I slide away from the counter. "I'm going to go check on the boys, see if they need any help."

"I'll come with ya."

We load our arms with beers because we know they'll want some too and make our way back out onto the patio where Winston, Foster, Sully, and—to my surprise—Porter are all lounging on chairs.

Riker's sleeping in Foster's arms, and they look so cute together.

"That's a good look for you," I say to him.

He grins down at my sleeping baby then sends a wink to his

fiancée. "I thought so too."

I glance between Foster and Wren, wondering if there's something there they aren't telling me.

I take a seat in one of the empty chairs, and it just so happens to be between Winston and Porter.

Awesome.

I hand Winston a beer. "Can you let me know when the meat is about ten minutes from being done? I'll start the mac and cheese then."

His brows lift and a slow grin starts over his lips.

"Don't you dare say a word," I hiss.

He chuckles, accepting the beer, but doesn't say anything.

"So, Drew," Porter says from my other side, and I turn toward him. "Wren tells me you're enjoying being a single mom. Is that true?"

I laugh at his candid question. "It's an…interesting experience. A little harder to navigate than I thought it'd be, but I'm making it work."

"Which part is your favorite? The shitty diapers, the constant drool, the crying, or the lack of sleep?"

"It's definitely the shitty diapers. I can live with those. The crying gives me a headache, the drool is disgusting and constant, and the lack of sleep makes me a raging bitch. Well, *more* of a raging bitch."

Porter laughs. "I do not miss those baby days one bit. I never want to go through that again."

"Really? You'd take the terrible twos over the baby days? I hear those are the worst."

"Oh, definitely. I have a really good *no* voice and Kyrie wasn't about to try to push my buttons." He leans into me. "My advice? Practice that voice now."

I chuckle. "Noted."

"So, uh, what's with the postnatal baby shower?"

"It's kind of a long story." I feel my cheeks heat, because the idea of it *does* sound silly, but I didn't have the time to have one before the baby came. I was too busy working myself to the bone to get ready for this new journey in my life.

"You realize you're supposed to have those *before* the baby is here, right? That's when you get all the good loot."

Winston chimes in. "That's exactly what I told her, but she doesn't listen for shit. She's stubborn."

"*She* can hear you," I say to him.

"*He* doesn't give a shit."

I turn back to Porter. "Sorry about him. He's the worst."

"He is *not* the worst," Winston insists.

"Lies."

"Bull."

"Cannot confirm."

Winston stares at Foster, Wren, and Sully, who all just turned on him in a heartbeat.

"What the fuck? You're all awful friends." He sits forward in his chair, reaching next to him and pinching Riker's cheek. "Except you. You're my best friend."

Foster pulls Riker away. "What the fuck am I? Chopped liver?"

"A traitor," Winston tells him. "With a little dick."

"Not true," Wren insists. "I can attest to this."

"Unfortunately," Sully says, "I can too." He looks to Foster, who's just grinning. "I can't believe you slept naked on the couch."

"I get night sweats," Foster argues. "Not my fault."

"Don't you dare blame your night sweats." Porter points at him. "You used to get naked *all* the time. You didn't even have to be drunk. You have zero humility."

"Wait a second." I sit forward. "Has *everyone* here seen Foster's dick besides me?"

They all nod, throwing out various affirmative responses.

"Well shit. I feel a little ripped off right now. Like, you all have this mutual bonding experience and I'm left in the dust."

"I mean, I can show you if you really want me to." Foster goes to stand, and I rush out of my chair, grabbing Riker.

"Give me my baby before you get naked."

His hands drop to the button on his jeans.

"Wait! Don't actually get naked!" I groan. "Oh my god. I can't believe I'm friends with you people."

"What do you mean 'you people'? We're fantastic," Wren says.

"You're something."

"I *am* fantastic," Porter insists. "You don't know me well enough to say otherwise yet."

"Fine. You get a pass. The rest of you suck."

None of them disagree.

"Here." Wren takes Riker out of my arms. "You sit. Let's open gifts before the food is ready. Also because I'm eager for you to see what I got you."

"That scares me."

"You're going to love it."

Wren settles down with Riker while Foster starts handing me gift bag after gift bag. There's a lot more here than there are people, which tells me they all went above and beyond to make this something special.

Which, I have to admit, I really appreciate, because my supplies are running low.

When I found out I was pregnant, I started buying things slowly every week. By the time he was here, I was stocked up for a while and didn't *need* the baby shower I didn't have time for.

I don't *need* it now, but Wren has been insisting for months that we do it, and since I've missed my friends lately, I agreed.

By the time I open the last bag, the deck is full of everything I could ever want, and not just the things he'll need during this stage of his life but items we'll use for years to come.

My heart feels so full I could burst.

I feel tears start to sting my eyes.

"Shit. I…I need to start the macaroni."

I race back into the house before they can see me cry.

I bypass the kitchen, knowing Wren will probably follow me inside. I just need a minute totally alone, so I close the door on the laundry room and let the tears finally fall.

There's a brute knock on the door and I jump from the sudden pounding against my back.

Before I can say anything, Winston shoulders his way inside.

He's so big and the room is so small. We're standing chest to chest when he closes the door.

"How'd you know I was in here?"

"Because I know you. You'd want somewhere quiet to cry, being all embarrassed and shit to show emotion in front of everyone. You headed this way, so I took a chance on you coming in here."

I wipe at my eyes. "Whatever."

"Why are you crying, Drew?"

"Because everyone is being so nice to me."

"I'm not."

I sniffle, laughing at his honesty. "True, but you could be."

"I could, but I like to think of our sparring matches as foreplay."

"Winston!"

"What?" he says innocently. "They basically are and you know it."

"They are not."

"Are too."

"Are not! There is nothing between us that's considered *foreplay*."

I try to push around him, but he doesn't budge.

"Let me out of here. I need to make your stupid mac and cheese."

"No."

"Yes. Move, Winston."

"No."

His hand comes up, covering my jaw, forcing me to look up into his eyes.

I'm stuck.

Not literally, but I couldn't move if I wanted to.

Not with the way he's looking at me.

One hand holding me steady, he trails his other down my arm, his fingertips dancing over my skin. His fingers circle my wrist and he places my hand on his body.

His chest.

His abs.

His hard cock.

"If our sparring matches aren't foreplay, explain this."

I gulp, loving the feel of him under my palm.

"Th-That's just you."

"It's not." He presses closer to me. "I know it's not."

"Is too."

"I could kiss you right now and you'd crumple into my arms. Don't tell me that's not true."

"It's not," I repeat. "That's not true at all."

His hand tightens on my jaw and he pulls my face closer…pulls my lips closer.

He knows what he's doing.

I know what he's doing…what he wants to do.

"This is your last warning, Drew…"

I don't say anything.

I let it happen.

Slice Twelve

WINSTON

I was right. She crumpled.

I had to wrap my arm around Drew's waist to keep her from falling as I claimed her mouth with my own.

I pull my lips from hers, running kisses across her jawline.

"See? I told you so."

I trail down her neck, biting at her sensitive skin and licking away the sting.

"I've thought about kissing you every single night since it first happened. You have no idea how badly I've wanted to pull you into me and not let you go until the sun came up."

She moans.

"You've thought about it too, haven't you?"

"Y-Yes. But, Winston?"

"What?"

"Shut the fuck up and keep kissing me."

I laugh against her, moving back to her lips. "Yes, ma'am."

She groans at my words, and the noise has my hips jutting forward, seeking any contact I can get from her.

I grab her ass cheeks, lifting her onto the dryer and pushing between her thighs and pulling her to the edge so I can feel her pussy on my cock.

I reach behind her for the controls.

"What are you doing?"

"Turning this on." I flip the switch.

"What?" She latches on to me when it kicks to life. "Why?"

"Because I'm about to make you come, and I'd rather they not hear us."

She gasps as I slide my hands into her hair and pull her toward me, crashing my lips to hers again.

They're soft.

I hate them and love them all at once.

She moves against me, needing all the same things I do, and I want to give them to her.

"Can I touch you?"

"Are you serious, Winston? If you don't touch me, I'm about to start touching myself."

"I'm confused. Is that a threat?" I drag my lips to her ear. "I've heard you touch yourself before, Drew, and I'd *love* to watch it."

Her breaths stutter. "You h-heard that?"

I nod. "I was on the other side of the door, doing the exact same thing."

"Were you really?"

"Yes."

"Shit," she mutters. "I think I just came."

"You didn't, but I can make it happen."

I slide my hands under her shirt, and she moans again.

"See? Aren't you glad I turned the dryer on?"

"I'll be glad when you actually make good on your promises."

Inching my hands up her body, I cup her breasts.

"If this is your idea of how to make me come, you're going the wrong way."

I cough out a laugh, pulling down the cups of her bra and rubbing my thumbs over her pebbled nipples. Her whole body tightens, and she presses her chest out, seeking more contact.

"You're so bossy when you're horny."

"Just when I'm horny?"

"Fair enough."

I take her mouth again, kissing her until she's writhing against me.

I kiss down her chin, her neck, over her collarbones until I'm at her breasts and close my mouth over her nipple, sucking it in.

She arches her back, clutching my shoulders tightly when I bite lightly.

"Fucking hell."

I grin and continue my assault on her tits until she's basically dry-humping me.

When I pull away, I can't tell if she's going to beg me to stay or murder me.

I grab her chin, pressing a fast kiss to her lips. "Undo your jeans."

She follows my instructions without breaking eye contact.

I don't break it either.

Not when I trace my fingers down her body.

Not when I slip my hand into her panties.

Not when my fingers slide between her wet, hot folds, finding her clit and rubbing gentle circles.

"Don't even think about it," I bark as she tries to close her eyes when the pressure becomes too much for her. "I want to watch you come apart."

"Then you better add another finger," she says, spreading her legs wider.

I dip two fingers into her pussy, resting my thumb against her clit. I don't even move my wrist and I can feel her begin to tighten at the invasion.

"Shit, shit, shit," she mumbles as she pants. "That feels so...*fuck*."

I chuckle and she swats, only to gasp at the angle I hit when she moves.

"Do that again," I tell her.

"What?"

"Ride my hand, Drew. Show me how you want to be touched."

Her movements are slow at first, unsure, but it doesn't take her long to find her rhythm.

Rubbing her clit as she gets herself off on my fingers, I cover her moans with my mouth, kissing them away so only I can hear them.

She wrenches her mouth from mine.

"I need to come."

"Whatever you need."

"Harder. Fuck me harder."

I do.

And before I know it, she's gasping softly, her body tightening around my fingers.

Her breaths come in short spurts as I ease my ministrations, letting her come down from the high she so desperately needed.

I pull my hand from her jeans and lean back, grinning.

"I—"

The laundry room door flies open, whacking me in the back, and I fall into Drew, using my body to shield her from the intruder.

"What the fuck?" I growl.

"Oh, shit. My bad." Foster's eyes move back and forth between me and Drew. "Oh. Well, hi, Drew."

She hides her face in my chest.

"What are you doing in here?"

"I, uh, heard the dryer. It wasn't on before and since I couldn't find you in the rest of the house…" He shrugs. "I took my chances."

"Get the fuck out, Foster!"

"I'm going, I'm going. By the way, Riker is awake, and he definitely shit. We drew straws and you lost, Drew."

"If I wasn't there to draw, how did I lose?" she asks, peeking around me.

"Exactly," he explains. "But, anyway, yeah. He's awake."

"Ugh," I groan. "Kids ruin everything. We'll be out in a sec."

Foster nods. "Roger that."

He backs out of the room, shutting the door and leaving us alone again.

"Aren't you glad you turned the dryer on?" Drew repeats my words back to me, grinning.

"Don't make me laugh right now. I'm trying to talk my boner down." Even so, I feel my lips pull into a grin.

"We should probably get back out there before anyone else gets curious."

I nod. "Good call."

I help her down from the dryer, my eyes falling to her chest.

"You might want to change your shirt."

She glances down at the two *very* wet spots I created. "Another good call."

Popping the dryer open, she bends to grab a shirt, and I have to force myself to look away because is it just me or does her ass look extra good in those jeans today?

She stands, ripping off her shirt and putting a new one on in its place.

"Were you checking me out?" she accuses.

"Yes, but I did just have my fingers in your pussy, so I think it's safe to say I'm allowed to do that."

She closes her eyes at my words, taking a deep breath.

"Not another word, Winston. Don't tell a soul."

"Don't tell a soul what? That you just came all over my hand?"

"Yes," she mutters through gritted teeth. "Keep your trap shut."

"Don't worry, Drew, I like to keep my conquests to myself."

"Good." She clears her throat, pushing her shoulders back. "And just so we're extra clear, this doesn't mean anything."

It does. "Whatever you say."

"Good," she repeats. "Now, if you'll excuse me, duty calls."

She brushes by me.

When her hand is on the doorknob, I grab her wrist.

"What?" she asks, looking down at where I'm touching her.

I like the way we look together, my suntanned skin against her own.

We're alike, yet so different.

I rub my fingers over her palm, loving how soft it feels.

"I, uh…"

She sighs. "Winston, I have to go. Whatever it is, we can talk about it later."

"Right. Later."

And I let her walk away.

Again.

I wait at least a minute before exiting the laundry room myself, surprised when I run into Foster, who's standing there waiting.

"What's up, man?" I ask casually.

"Look, it's not my business, but I just wanted to say…please don't hurt her. She's Wren's best friend. I don't want to have to choose sides if this all goes south."

My stomach feels like it's been punched.

Foster's my best friend. He knows me better than anyone.

Does he really think so little of me? Think I'd hurt Drew on purpose?

I grind my teeth, my jaw throbbing from how hard I have my molars pressed together.

"I don't mean it in a bad way, Win. I just know you. You aren't exactly known for being a commitment kind of guy. You're just…well, you, and Drew is in a tough spot right now with Riker and everything else going on in her life. Don't—"

"What?" I seethe. "Take advantage of her emotional state? Is that what you think of me?"

He shakes his head, holding his hands up, trying to soothe me. "No, no, I don't. You know I don't. I'm just saying make sure you're both on the same page about what you're doing. I'm just trying to look out for everyone involved."

"Mostly your own balls," I say.

He laughs. "Well, kind of. But also everyone." He hooks his thumb over his shoulder. "I'm gonna go help Wren finish getting everything ready. Might wanna, uh, wash your hands. Dinner's done."

Foster gives me one last long look before turning and leaving me in the hallway alone.

He's wrong.

This isn't some one-off for me. It's not a fling, not something I'm just randomly acting on.

I like Drew—a lot more than I'm willing to admit to her or anyone else.

Sure, she drives me insane, but that's nothing new. Everyone drives me insane.

But she also calls me on my shit. She doesn't want me to waste away into nothing. She pushes me. Annoys me, yes, but pushes me. To be better. To be something more.

I hate it, and I love it.

I hate *her*, and I think I could love her.

If she'd let me.

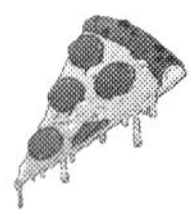

"Shhh." I pat the back of a screaming Riker. This seems to be a new thing with us, me getting up in the middle of the night to care for him.

I'm not complaining by any means, because it's not like I sleep that well anyway.

I wouldn't admit this to anyone, but I enjoy our time together. Even with all his wailing and waking me up in the middle of the night, Riker is a pretty cool little dude.

"Go back to sleep, buddy. It was just a bad dream is all."

I walk him around the room for several minutes in an attempt to settle him down. My shoulder is aching with his weight, but I push through it like I always do for him.

"That's right, close those tired little peepers. Get some shut-eye for all our sakes."

After what feels like ages, he starts to quiet, and I make my way to the crib he loves so much.

It makes me happy that something as simple as my poorly crafted mobile can bring such a smile to his face.

"I thought you didn't like babies."

I turn toward the bed. Drew's lying on her side, watching us.

"I don't."

"It seems to me you like Riker."

I place him gently into his bed, patting his belly as he fights with all his might to keep his sleepy eyes open.

"He's an exception."

"It's the ginger hair and bright eyes, isn't it? Makes him irresistible."

"How the fuck did he end up with red hair?"

She chuckles. "Beats me. Nobody in my family has it as far as I know. Must be from Chadwick's side somewhere."

"That asshole wasn't a ginger, right?" She shakes her head. "That's how I thought I remembered him."

"Remembered him?" Drew sits up. "I never brought him into Slice…"

Oh fuck.

"You sure about that? I—"

"I'm positive, Winston." She crosses her arms over her chest, pushing her tits up, my attention falling to her rack. "Don't play games with me."

I push away from the crib, squaring my shoulders and readying myself for this fight, because it's going to be a long one.

"It's the middle of the night. Do we really want to do this now?"

"Yes. I want to do this now," she insists.

"Fine, then we should probably move this somewhere else so we don't wake Riker."

She doesn't say anything, just shoves up from the bed and stomps into the living room.

Well, this is going to be fun.

I don't trudge her way immediately, dragging my feet at the dresser, delaying this knockdown drag-out as much as I can.

When I finally make it into the living room, she's fuming.

I can see it in her eyes. They look almost black at this point.

"What did you mean by that's how you remembered him?" she says right away. "When did you meet Chadwick? Did you—"

She pauses, angry eyes raking over me.

"Winston, did you just change your outfit?"

"Yes."

"What? Why?"

"I read online that girls can't resist a guy when he's wearing gray sweatpants and a white t-shirt." I shrug. "If we're gonna fight, might as well shoot for some mind-blowing makeup sex afterward."

She's furious, standing there arms crossed, foot a-tappin' away, not even caring about my brilliant stroke of genius.

Oh, boy. I'm in for it now.

"Tell me how you know him."

"We talked."

"What does that mean? Elaborate for me. Talk to me like I'm really dumb and spell it out."

"It means *I*"—I stab at my chest—"did what you didn't have the fucking balls to do, okay? I told that sad sack of shit to walk out of your life and Riker's if he wasn't going to fully be in it. I told him to fuck off for you."

Her mouth drops open.

Closed.

Open.

Closed.

"Are you fucking serious?" she explodes, storming toward me. She beats at my chest with her tiny fists. "Why, Winston? Why would you do that? How could you? I—"

"Because!" I scream back, grabbing her shoulders and holding her still. She stares up at me with wide, frightened eyes. "Because," I repeat softer. "Do you have any idea how excruciating it was to watch you come into work day after fucking day, your belly growing bigger and your tears lasting longer? Do you have any clue how much it killed me to watch you break apart over that tool?" I grab her chin. "How much I wanted to rescue you?"

She pushes out of my hold. "I don't *need* rescuing, Winston. It wasn't your place to say anything to him. What happened between us was *my* business. You had no right."

"Maybe you're right," I say. "Maybe it wasn't my place, but I did you a favor and we both know it."

"Riker is going to grow up without a dad because of you."

"Bullshit. You don't have to be a kid's biological father to be a dad to them. That's not how it works. And because of what I did, he's going to grow up with the dad he deserves. You and I both know it."

She glances away, because she knows I'm right.

I saved her the grief of having to do it herself. She should be thanking me, not bitching at me.

"You still had no right."

"I didn't, but I'm not going to apologize for helping you, Drew, just like I won't apologize for getting you out of that shitty apartment or paying for your car. It's just not going to happen. Get over it."

"I don't need your help," she says forcefully. "Stop trying to save me."

"You can't expect me to stop doing that."

"Why the fuck not?"

"Because I care, okay?" I shout. "I fucking care about you!"

She stumbles back, mouth dropped open in shock.

"Why is that such a surprise to you?" I push.

"Because you don't care about anything."

"That's not true. I care about a lot."

"Not anything that matters."

"I care about you."

"Stop saying that," she urges.

"Why? It's the truth."

"It's not. You're just saying it."

"Why would I just say it? What motivations do I have?"

She waves her hand up and down. "You literally just changed your entire outfit in hopes of getting me to sleep with you. Your intentions are very clear right now, so I don't believe a word coming out of your mouth."

"Are you serious?" I ask.

"Yes! This is what blows my mind when it comes to you, Winston. You think so far ahead that you change your outfit in hopes of getting me in the sack, but you can't be bothered to do something about your future to make sure you're always covered and not just working in your father's pizzeria the rest of your life."

"What's so wrong with that plan? That's what you want to do."

"Yes, but that's entirely different. I *love* cooking, love creating new, weird dishes, and I just happen to love pizza. Working my way into the kitchen at Slice is the perfect job for me to start with, but you have zero interest in any of it. Why are you still there?"

"That's not true," I dispute. "I love pizza."

She growls, clearly irritated with me right now. "You know what I mean, Winston."

"I do." I nod. "I do know what you mean, but what I don't get is why it's so fucking important to *you* for me to do something with *my* life. You got a heart-on for me too?"

"No, I don't have a hard-on for you. I—"

"I didn't say hard-on. We both already know I make you horny as fuck, Drew. I said *heart*-on. Do you *care* about me too?"

Her eyes flit away when I say this, and I know the next words to leave her mouth are going to be complete and utter bullshit.

"No."

"Liar," I say, calling her on it. "You're lying."

"I am not," she avers. "I don't have a heart-on for you."

"You do." I stalk toward her, grasping her chin in my hand,

pulling her attention to me because I want her to see the look in my eyes. "You care. You don't want to because I drive you crazy because I don't have my shit together, but you still fucking care."

"Shut up, Winston," she grumbles, trying to twist out of my hold, but I don't let her move. "I don't care."

Instead, I yank her toward me, wrapping my arm around her waist and trapping her there. "Yes, you do. Admit it."

"No."

"Admit it. Say it and I'll let you go."

"N-No." She tries to hold firm, but her voice waivers.

"Unless you don't *want* me to let you go." I pull her chin up, closer to my lips. "What do you want? Do you want me to let you go…let *this* go? Or do you want *me*?"

She knows I'm referring to our first kiss.

There's no doubt in my mind that if I hadn't stopped us, Drew would have let me lay her down and have my way with her.

But I knew things would be different if we crossed that line.

Just like now.

She wants me to touch her again. She's craving it.

She's just not sure she's ready for the impact it'll have if we give in.

"I-I…I don't know," she whispers.

"Yes, you do. You're just afraid to say it. But you *need* to say it."

She gulps, and I lean closer, our lips almost touching now.

"Do you want me, Drew? Or do you want *this*?"

She closes her eyes. "Y-You."

"Open your eyes and look at me."

Her brown gaze collides with my blues.

"Say it again."

"You." She sighs in relief, and her body sags against mine. "I want *you*."

Slice Thirteen

DREW

"I want *you*."

The second the words leave my lips, his mouth is on mine.

The kiss is hard and soft and slow and fast all at once.

I could kiss him forever.

If he weren't so stupid.

Of course I care about him. How could I not? He's wormed his way into my head, and somehow my heart too. It scares me how much I think about him now.

How much I think I could want him. *Need* him.

I pull away.

"I'm not done being mad at you," I warn. "This doesn't change that fact."

"When are you not mad at me?"

He tries to pull me back to him, but I don't let him.

"I still hate you."

Meaning this is *just sex*. No strings.

"I still hate you too," he says in understanding, and then he's taking my mouth once more.

His tongue traces along my lips and I open for him, our mouths dancing together like they're old friends.

I trace my hands up his chest, loving the way he feels under my palms. His chest is so defined, muscles taut as he holds me tightly against his body. His cock rubs against my belly, and it feels so hard. So heavy.

I need to know how he tastes.

I don't think, just drop to my knees, pulling those stupid sexy sweats down along the way.

"What the…*uhhhh*…"

His words turn into a moan as I run my tongue over his skin.

Up and down, over and over, using my spit to coat his length.

To tease him.

His hands crash into my hair and he lifts it into a pile on my head, pulling it to get my attention.

I glance up at him.

"I wish I were one of those dudes who had the ability to be all chill about it, saying you don't have to do this if you don't want to, but fuck. You on your knees? Looking up at me like you are?" He hisses. "Please, for the love of all things holy, suck my cock already, Drew. You're killing me."

I heed his instructions, pulling his hard length into my mouth, loving having him at my mercy.

But more than that, I love the feel of him on my tongue.

Inch by inch, I take him until I can feel myself starting to gag and back off.

"Do that again."

I do, only this time he holds me there, not letting me move. I can feel his cock sitting there, pulsing. My mouth feels like it's stretched beyond capacity and I can't breathe.

He trails one hand down the side of my face to my jaw, rubbing it.

"Relax for me," he coaches. "Relax and breathe through your nose."

I do as he says and feel him push deeper.

"That's it," he approves. "Fucking hell."

With no warning, he wrenches himself from my mouth, pulling me up.

He strips my camisole from my body, and my first reaction is to wrap my arms around my waist.

Pregnancy wasn't kind to my skin, and I was left with what seems like hundreds of tiny little stretch marks all across my stomach.

"What are you doing?" He tugs my makeshift shield away. "Don't hide yourself from me."

"I have stretch marks."

He scowls. "Big fucking deal. We all have scars." He runs his fingertips over my imperfections. "Some of them are just more beautiful than others."

He skates his fingers up my body and flicks the button on my front-clasping bra, my tits falling free.

His blue eyes darken as he watches them bounce, his lip captured between his teeth.

"Do you trust me?" he asks, searching my eyes.

"Yes."

The response is automatic but sincere.

"Stay here." He pulls his sweats over his erection and disappears into the bedroom, returning just seconds later with a camera in hand. "If you're not comfortable with this, tell me, but you have no fucking idea how insanely hot you look right now, and I want you to see it. I want you to see how perfect you are."

He wants to take my picture? Now?

My first instinct is to say no.

I mean, I'm not stupid. I've heard the horror stories from others. Those photos could wind up anywhere.

But this is Winston.

He wouldn't hurt me. All he wants to do is save me.

"Take it," I tell him before I can back out.

The sound of his camera shutter fills the otherwise quiet room.

I just stand here, unsure what to do.

He peeks at me over the lens, that same hunger still in his eyes. "You're so fucking gorgeous, Drew."

The way he's looking at me…I almost believe him.

He snaps a few more photos, then sets his camera on the living room table.

"Get on the couch and spread your legs."

I all but rip my shorts down, stumbling my way to the cushions.

Winston stays where he is, hand on his cock, watching me as I open my thighs for him.

Waiting.

"Wider."

I go wider.

"Don't fucking play games with me, Drew. I said wider."

My cheeks flush, but I do it.

I've never been so exposed in front of a guy before.

I'm embarrassed, but with the way Winston's staring at me like I'm his next meal, I'm excited.

Slowly, he ambles toward me, taking his time, fingers still wrapped around his cock.

Holding my stare, he drops to his knees, and my clit pulses with anticipation as he lowers his head.

Only he doesn't bury his face between my legs like I hoped he would.

Instead, he kisses my stomach.

He kisses my scars.

He kisses away all my insecurities.

Kisses my heart.

Just when I think it couldn't get any better, he kisses my clit, and I nearly combust at the soft, simple touch.

He peers up at me, blue eyes still ablaze.

"I'm going to eat your pussy now, Drew."

He braces a hand on each thigh, pushing my legs apart even farther, and *finally* tastes me for real.

I melt into oblivion.

Or the couch.

They both feel the same right now.

His licks are slow, purposeful. He takes his time teasing me, lavishing me. He switches between gentle strokes, sucking my clit into his mouth, and flicking his tongue against me like he's tapping it.

Every time I think I'm about to explode, he walks me off the ledge, pulling away and dipping his tongue into my opening, only to start all over again.

I've never had someone eat me out with such attention before.

"Winston…" I whine. "Let me come."

He laughs, and the vibration against my clit feels fucking magical.

"Fine, but only because I'm selfish and can't wait another minute to feel your pussy wrapped around my dick."

This time, he lets me leap over the ledge.

And I soar.

Higher than I've ever soared before.

When I've finally fallen back to earth, Winston sits back on his haunches, wiping his mouth with the back of his hand. He grabs my hands, helping me stand. Then he turns me around, gently pushing me toward the cushions. I fall onto my knees, bracing my hands on the back of the couch as I listen to him get rid of his sweats and his shirt.

I gasp as I feel his hard cock brush against my ass when he situates himself behind me.

"I'm going to fuck you hard and fast, Drew. Next time, I'll take my time inside you."

I nod.

"Are you sure you're okay with this?"

"Winston, I just spread my legs wider than I did to birth my son and let you eat my pussy for fifteen minutes. I think we're beyond being okay with this."

He chuckles, nibbling at my shoulder. "Fair enough."

The head of his cock pushes against my hole and he lets out a string of cuss words as he starts to stretch me.

I groan as he slowly—painfully slowly—pushes all the way in.

"I thought you promised this would be hard and fast. This feels weak and slow to me."

He growls at my smartass comment, his fingers digging into my ass cheeks so hard I'm sure they'll be bruised tomorrow, and he starts pumping into me just like he promised.

Having Winston inside me is unlike anything I've felt before.

It feels good. Too good.

Like the kind of good I could get really used to really fast.

We find a rhythm, our thighs slapping together so loudly that there is no way Sully doesn't hear us.

But I don't care.

In this moment, all I care about is this.

Because nothing will ever be this good again.

"I wasn't kidding about this being fast," Winston cautions. "I'm really close."

"I don't care. I am too."

"Touch yourself," he tells me, biting at my shoulder again. "Rub your clit."

I do, and I feel him start to tighten.

"Don't pull out," I say. "I'm on birth control."

"Shit! Fuck!" His pace slows. "I forgot a condom."

"I don't care. I'm clean."

"I am too."

I know he is. I know he wouldn't dare enter me if he weren't clean. I trust him.

His pace quickens again, and I rub short circles over my clit, chasing that high for the second time tonight.

The orgasm hits me out of nowhere, and my pulsing pussy is enough to send Winston over the edge too as he slams into me harder than before, burying himself to the hilt and filling me with his cum.

"Motherfucker," he mutters, resting his head between my shoulder blades, his breaths coming in short spurts.

"Literally," I say.

He laughs. "Shut up."

We rest for a minute, letting our breathing return to normal, then untangle ourselves from the mess we're in.

We don't say anything as I toss my camisole back over my head and pull my underwear back on, trying to keep my legs as closed as possible. I can already feel the evidence of what we just did dripping between my thighs.

We're silent as he pulls his sweats back on, tucking his softening cock away.

The reality of what just happened between us is setting in, and I can't help but wonder if he's regretting it.

I'm not, though I wish I were.

It would make it easier when I leave.

Make it so I don't want it again, but I already do.

I glance over at Winston, and he grins at me.

"What?" I ask, unable to stop my lips from pulling up at the corners.

"It was totally the gray sweats, wasn't it?"

I can still feel him the next morning.

My muscles are tender, ass cheeks aching from where he dug his fingers into me, and my vagina feels like it was fucked…*hard.*

And yet, I love every single sensation.

"I had the craziest dream last night," Winston says, crawling back into bed after brushing his teeth and checking on Riker, who is still sound asleep at eight AM. "You got mad at me for doing you a total solid, and then you called me a lazy piece of shit. You sucked my cock, I ate your pussy, and then we fucked—*raw.*" He rubs his hand over his face. "What a wild night."

I smack his naked chest. "Shut up, you ass."

"Come on," he coaxes, rolling over me until I'm pinned under him, fitting himself between my legs like he belongs there. And, okay, maybe he does, and the confidence he exudes is enough to awaken a throbbing between my legs. "Let's do it again."

"Let's not."

"Why? You can't tell me it wasn't good."

"How would I know? It was just a dream."

He pushes his already hard dick into me. "You're a tease."

"No, a tease would wake you up with a blow job and then not let you finish. I'm not *that* mean."

"I mean, you *did* suck my cock last night and not let me come in your mouth."

"That was entirely on you, buddy."

He narrows his eyes at me. "Fine. You win this round." He presses a quick kiss to my lips. "What's on the agenda today? I mean, after morning sex and all."

"Well, first, there will be no morning sex. Second, *we* have to work."

He groans, rolling off me.

Pop.

There is no mistaking that the noise coming from his body didn't sound right.

"Winston? What the fuck was that?"

He's lying there, jaw clenched, cradling his shoulder.

"It was nothing," he lies.

"Nothing never means nothing," I say, repeating his words back to him. "Tell me what's wrong."

"It's just my shoulder."

"Obviously," I say, sitting up. "What exactly is wrong with it?"

"It's not a big deal." He rolls away from me. "It just does that sometimes."

"It *is* a big deal." I pull at him, trying to get him to roll back my way. "Come on."

"No."

"Yes. Talk to me."

"Stop!" he yells.

I freeze.

He glowers at me. "Just fucking stop. Leave it alone."

Slowly, I pull my hands away. "Okay."

He stares straight ahead, and I know he regrets his yelling

instantly and wants to apologize.

He knows it won't do any good.

Instead, he leans over. I turn away from his kiss, and it lands on my cheek.

He sighs, head resting against my temple. "I'm gonna go shower."

His voice is hushed, like he's trying to make up for shouting without actually saying he's sorry.

But it's not enough. We both know it.

When I don't respond, he pushes from the bed with one last lingering look and shuts himself into the bathroom.

I don't breathe again until I hear the water turn on.

I want to storm in there after him. I want to force him to tell me what's wrong. I want to help him. I *need* to help him.

Just like he needed to help me.

It's not fair that he gets to butt into my life when I don't want him to but I can't butt into his.

He said things would be different after, but this feels an awful lot like more of the same.

Before I can talk myself out of it, I pop off the bed and charge into the bathroom like he's done to me so many times now.

I jerk open the shower curtain.

"What the—" He jumps, and I try hard not to let my eyes drop to his cock.

"You said it's supposed to be different now. This isn't fucking different, Winston."

"I said different between *us*, as in we know what the other looks like naked now. But this is *my* business, Drew. Not yours."

"You put your dick inside of me *without* protection. You made *your* business *my* business in that moment. That isn't a line you cross with just anyone."

He doesn't say anything.

He knows I'm right.

"Now, for one time in your life, will you *please* just stop being so damn annoying and tell me what's going on with you? It's bad, isn't it?" I ask.

"Hurts a little more than usual."

"Usual? Does it pop like that often?"

"More than it should."

"Winston, you *have* to go get it looked at. You cannot live your life this way. It's just not realistic. It makes zero sense to me why you feel this insane need to take care of me and not yourself too."

He sneers. "Because I don't want to be a slave to the medical system."

"Well tough!" I bellow. "Fucking tough. You don't always get to do what you *want* to do. You buckle up and act like a goddamn grown-up. Do you think I *wanted* to raise myself? Do you think I *wanted* to have to learn how to pay bills when I was ten so we would have water and electricity because I was tired of going to school dirty and getting made fun of? Do you think I *wanted* to starve for days so we could save a little extra cash at the end of the week to float us by until payday just in case something came up? Do you think I *wanted* to get pregnant by some douchebag and raise a baby alone? No, Winston! I didn't want any of that shit, but it's what life handed me. So, I pulled up my britches and made fucking do." I sigh. "That's what being a grown-up is—being responsible *especially* when you don't want to."

He stares at me, eyes full of pity and sorrow.

Maybe even a little acceptance.

"I don't want to be a grown-up," he says quietly, his voice rough like he's trying to choke back emotion.

I laugh softly. "It's funny—we want to grow up so fast when we're young, want to get to do all the things we can't as children, but no one ever warns you how exhausting it is to be older."

"So exhausting. I'm tired all the time."

"Me too. Can I ask you something though?"

"I mean, I'm not really in a position to run away from you right now."

"True." *Don't look at his dick. Don't look at his dick.*

"It's okay to look at my dick, Drew. I know you want to."

I try to roll my eyes and be annoyed, but instead I smile. "Shut up. Did you actually finish physical therapy?"

"Sure did."

I narrow my eyes, because there's something in the way he says it. It's…off.

"Winston…were you *ready* to finish it? Truly ready? Or did you just give up because things weren't happening as fast as you would have liked?"

"I could use my camera again. It's all the therapy I need."

"And the weed."

His lips twist, like he has something to say but doesn't want to say it.

"What?" I push.

"I actually haven't smoked since I said those…unkind things to you."

"Unkind? You mean cruel? Harsh? Wicked? Ruthless?"

His thick brows slam down. "What are you, a thesaurus?"

"I'm just stating the truth."

He grumbles something I can't make out then says, "Can you just come in here with me? It's cold as fuck with the curtain open and I'd rather we be on even ground than have you standing there judging me."

I raise my brows at him.

"No funny business," he promises.

"For the record," I say, pulling my camisole over my head and shimmying my undies down my legs, "I wasn't judging you."

He curls an arm around my waist once I'm inside the tub, yanking me to him until we're plastered together.

He stares down at me, his eyes darting between my lips and my eyes, mouth moving closer to mine by the second.

Licking my lips in anticipation, I want nothing more than for him to kiss me in this moment.

But at the last instant, he goes left, locking his other arm around me, burrowing his face into the crook of my neck.

He's hugging me.

His grip is tight. Hard.

It feels like so much more than a hug.

Like he'll never let me go.

I weave my arms around him, holding him to me like I never *want* him to let me go.

"I'm sorry. I know you hate it when I say that because you think I don't mean it, but I do. I'm just…I don't know. I'm scared."

"Of what, Winston?"

"What if something is really wrong with me? What if they can't fix my body? What if I'm just supposed to be this way now? What if one day I wake up and can't even lift my camera?"

"I don't believe that'll happen."

"The therapy didn't work before, so it could."

"Did you really put in the effort? Or did you just give up when it wasn't fixed right away?" I ask again, because he didn't give me a straight answer before.

His eyes dart to the side. Then he takes a breath, like he needs courage to speak again.

"I gave up," he admits, voice full of remorse and resentment.

"Then don't give up. Go back. See what they can do. Maybe you don't have to live like this."

"What if I do?"

"Then we'll figure it out."

We don't say anything for a while, just stand here under the water, letting it rain down on us, holding each other, being together.

"You said we," Winston mutters after several minutes.

I gulp. "I did."

I feel him smile against me. "It's because I can eat a mean pussy, isn't it?"

"Winston!" I try to pull away, smacking at him, but he doesn't let me get far.

"I'm kidding, I'm kidding."

He pulls me back into him, grabbing my chin and holding me still. He peers down at me, eyes full of appreciation and something I can't quite place.

"Thank you, Drew."

"Don't thank me yet…"

I drop to my knees.

"Oh, hell yes," he says, not even trying to hide his excitement as he leans against the wall in anticipation.

I can't help but laugh at him.

"Oh, sorry, I was just grabbing this bottle of shampoo you dropped." I stand, holding a bottle I obviously plucked from its perfectly safe spot on the shelf. "Saved your life. Now you can thank me."

He pushes off the wall, looking sour at my fake-out. "You're evil."

"What?" I blink innocently. "Oh…" I put one hand to my throat. "Did you think I was gonna give you a blow job?"

His eyes narrow into slits. "You knew what you were doing."

"You know, you should really think of upgrading your shower. Maybe get one of those fancy standup ones with a blow job bench. We could get some good use out of it."

He sputters, laughing hard. "You know that's not what it's called, right?"

"Come on. *Nobody* uses those things for anything other than blow jobs or oral. That's just not practical at all. It's absurd. Downright moronic."

"You telling me if I got a blow job bench, you'd use it on me?"

"I'm saying if you got a blow job bench, it would be used." I lift a shoulder. "We'll see if I'm the one on my knees or not."

Slice Fourteen

WINSTON

Winston's To-Do List:

Set up appointment with contractor for a new shower…with a blow job bench.

Slice Fifteen

DREW

I'm starting to believe I'm trapped in a parallel universe or something because I can't seem to keep my hands off Winston.

I want to touch him, not just punch him.

I want to be *around* him. Want to argue with him. Laugh with him. Simply sleep next to him.

I just want to…*be* with him.

It's…weird, yet exciting.

And *so* fucking scary.

I'm sixty percent sure the spike in my libido over the last few days is because I'm making up for lost time—AKA being pregnant and single for so long—but it's that forty percent that keeps nagging at me.

Maybe it *is* just Winston.

Maybe I'm not stuck in a parallel universe.

Maybe…I like him.

It's something I thought was impossible, but perhaps I was wrong.

Since living with him, I've seen a side of him I never paid any attention to before.

He's not the lazy asshole he seems to let everyone think he is. In fact, he's quite the opposite. Thoughtful in ways I didn't expect, he's always doing small things for me, like making sure I have a clean towel when I get out of the shower and letting me get a plate of food first after slaving over a hot stove.

I've learned a lot about his habits too.

He's an early riser, which surprised the hell out of me the first time he took off before the sunrise to capture it on film. He is fiercely protective of and dedicated to his hobby, and the time he devotes to it blows me away.

If someone were to twist my arm, I might actually admit Winston isn't the bad guy I've made him out to be.

I just wish he'd give his body and his responsibilities the same attention he gives his photography.

"What are you thinking about?" Winston asks, sliding the back door closed. "I swear I can hear your thoughts inside." He flops down into the lounger next to me. "Here," he says. "Thought you could use this."

He's holding out a pint of ice cream.

"What's this for?" I ask, taking the offering because, though I didn't ask for it, I'm not insane enough to pass up free ice cream.

"When you're not trying to jump my bones or give me random blow jobs in the kitchen, you've been kind of…off. I know you're not on your period, but something's up. Ice cream always makes me feel better, so I figured it could work for you too."

I smile, and my heart pitter-patters like it does when I look at my son.

It feels full.

"*You* try to jump my bones too," I defend, twisting off the ice cream lid.

And he might think I don't notice, but I am well aware he always initiates something sexual whenever I bring up him trying physical therapy again.

I let it slide, because he won't go until he's ready to go.

I've said what I needed to say about it. Pushing him will do no good.

"True, but I'm just a horny, irresponsible twentysomething-year-old with nothing else to do but fuck. What's your excuse?"

I don't have one.

"Thanks for this." I shake the ice cream at him, ignoring his question. "You forgot a spoon though."

"Ah, one moment." He grabs one out of his pocket and hands it to me. "I thought of everything."

"You're really trying to butter me up."

He takes a sip of the beer he went inside for in the first place. "I'm just trying to figure out why it sometimes feels like you're hate-fucking me and others it feels like there's something else there."

I nearly choke on the bite of ice cream sliding down my throat.

Good thing this stuff melts easily.

"Jesus, Winston," I say, wiping my mouth. "Tell me how you really feel."

"You couldn't handle how I really feel."

He tips the bottle back to his lips, and I know he can feel my eyes on him.

Neither of us address his statement, because we both know he's probably right.

"I'm not hate-fucking you." He slides his eyes my way, and I chuckle. "Okay, maybe a little, but you had it coming."

"Fair enough," he agrees. "What about the other times though? What's going on?"

What's going on is that I think I might have feelings for you, and I don't want *to have feelings for you.*

But I don't say that because I'm way too afraid of his reaction.

I don't get easily intimidated. It's just not who I am, probably from my hard upbringing, and I don't let anyone or anything get the best of me.

Winston, though…he's different.

He scares me, and I don't know why.

I sigh, setting my ice cream on the table next to me, and turn toward him.

"What are we doing, Winston?"

"Well, I'm enjoying this beer." He takes another sip. "And you're enjoying your free ice cream while we both enjoy this insanely beautiful night with zero dirty diapers because my sister kidnapped your baby."

"You know what I mean," I press.

He downs the rest of his beer and sets the bottle aside. For a few minutes, he doesn't say anything. Just sits there, watching the coastline while I watch him.

I wish I could crawl inside his head and figure out what he's thinking, because it looks important.

Then he rolls his head toward me, his usually bright blue eyes looking like sapphires in the glow of the setting sun.

"Look, Drew, I don't know what we're doing right now. I don't know what any of what we've been doing the last week means, but I do know I don't want to talk about it right now. Right now, I want to touch you. Right now, I want you to come over here and ride my face and my cock until the sun comes up. We can figure out everything else later."

Just the mention of his cock has me missing the feel of him inside me.

Missing the feel of him inside me? What the fuck is wrong with me? Who have I become?

"Drew."

My eyes snap to his.

He's staring at me with this…hunger. Like he hasn't eaten in days.

Suddenly, I want him to take his fill.

"Come here."

I stand, and he scoots down in the chair, patting the wide lounger arms.

"Rest your knees here."

I bite my lip, looking at the arms that are just wide enough for me to balance on but are hard enough that I know I'm going to have bruises tomorrow.

I've felt his tongue on me before.

They'll be worth it.

I throw my leg over him, using the back of the chair as support and resting my knees on the arms.

Winston's hands trace up my thighs, pushing the hem of my long t-shirt—one of his, of course—up my legs, revealing my uncovered pussy.

The night breeze is chilly on my skin, and I worry for a second about someone else being out on their porch, watching us, but the thought passes as quickly as it comes.

I want this too bad to care.

"My, my. You've been going commando this whole time?"

I lift a shoulder. "Riker isn't here, and Sully is conveniently gone too. I didn't see the point in panties."

He grins at me, approving of my decision.

He pushes the shirt up around my waist, his thumbs stroking my stretch marks in a loving manner.

No matter how many times Winston has seen me naked over the last few days, he's always taken time to show my scars attention, and every time, it makes my heart flutter.

Don't get me wrong, the sex with Winston is incredible.

But it's the small moments, like when he kisses my scars or when he helps me with Riker, that make me feel like there's something more going on inside his head.

That make *me* feel something.

I'm not stupid enough to mix feelings and sex again. I did that before with Chadwick. I thought for sure when I told him I was pregnant things would be different between us, and I guess in a sense I was right because he basically disappeared, but nothing went as planned.

Mixing sex and feelings got me single and alone, broke and living with my nemesis.

It's not a mistake I'll make again.

This is *just* sex. It has to be.

Right?

"Hold your shirt up," he directs.

I do, and he uses his thumbs to spread my folds open.

"God, you're so gorgeous," he murmurs, eyes firmly on my bare pussy. "So fucking perfect."

He leans forward, and I brace myself, so ready to feel his tongue on me again.

He hasn't eaten me out since the first night we slept together, and

I've been craving it since.

Only instead of flicking his tongue out, he places a gentle kiss to my clit.

I groan in frustration and he chuckles.

"So impatient," he teases.

"Well, yeah," I huff. "This chair fucking hurts."

"Does it?" He grabs my thighs, holding me steady and tightly, my hips canting just half an inch closer to him with how strongly he's gripping me. "Well then you better hurry up and fuck my face, Drew, because that's the only way you're getting down."

I don't know what's wrong with me, because I would *never* just heed a command like this, especially something so carnal, but in this moment I don't care.

I fuck him.

I was right to miss this, because the way his tongue feels on my pussy is pure fucking magic.

He makes me come twice before the ache in my knees becomes too much to bear.

Winston helps me down onto the lounger, laying my spent form on top of him.

"Holy hell," I say breathlessly. "That was…*wow*."

"You're welcome."

I pinch his nipple. "Shut up."

He kisses the top of my head, and I close my eyes, sinking into his warmth.

He runs his hands over my exposed ass, kneading my cheeks, his fingers playing along my crack.

"Don't even think about it. It's not happening. That's a no-go zone."

He laughs. "I'll talk you into it one day."

"Good luck," I say to him, my body feeling so tired and worn out from all the sex over the last several days. "I'm sleepy."

"Then nap. I'll wake you up in a bit."

When I peel my eyes open again, it's dark out.

The crickets chirp back and forth, creating an arrangement only they can understand. The waves of the ocean lap against the shore, and the night air shifts with a cool breeze like no other.

It's peaceful and melodic.

I could get used to sitting out here listening to the music the coast makes.

Don't get ahead of yourself, Drew. This isn't permanent.

I might be staying with Winston for now, but nothing about this is going to be long term. It's just until I can get on my feet again.

I can't get attached to any of it.

Especially not him.

"Oh my god, finally," Winston says from behind me when I stretch my back. "You're awake."

Somehow during our nap, we moved until we were spooning.

And based on the hard, hot cock I feel poking against my ass, Winston lost his shorts.

"I didn't realize when you said you'd wake me in a bit, it would be for sex."

"Did you expect anything less?" Winston's lips ghost over my ear and he drives his hips into me. "Hey, Drew, you want some fuck?"

I bust into laughter, shaking my head. "You are a complete idiot. A total moron. A horri—*mmmm.*"

A moan slips out as his tongue slides over that sensitive spot just under my ear.

"What was that? Something about how horrible I am?"

"Shut up. Just…"

His tongue dances along the spot again and I squeeze my thighs together, the touch going right between them.

"Just what?" he whispers. "Just fuck you already?"

I nod. "But dibs on bottom. My knees hurt too bad to be on top."

His hand runs up the back of my thigh, and to my surprise, he lifts it until my calf is resting on the same arm that gave me bruises I'll cherish.

Adjusting himself on the lounger, he snakes his hand between my thighs and slides his fingers between my folds, finding my clit, stroking it just the way he knows I like it.

He plays with me long enough to get me standing on the edge then dips two fingers inside, stretching me.

When I'm good and ready, he guides his cock into me.

Winston takes his time fucking me. His thrusts are slow. Short. Lazy even.

By the time he's getting close, I feel like I'm about to explode.

"I need to come," I say to him, practically whining.

"Again? You're so greedy," he teases. "Can you stand being on your knees for a minute?"

"For an orgasm after you've been torturing me for so long? Yes."

Laughing, he pulls out of me, and I miss the feeling instantly.

I wonder if I'll always feel that way when he leaves me.

Will I ever be the same after we're done doing whatever it is we're doing? Am I going to be able to walk away from this—from *him*—when it's all over?

No feelings, no feelings, no feelings.

If I say it enough times, I'll believe it.

Winston adjusts us until I'm on my knees and he's behind me, sliding back in like he was made to fit me.

Then he fucks me.

Hard.

So hard my knees aren't the only place I'll be feeling it tomorrow.

His fingers play against my clit as he pounds into me, and I fall apart around him.

He falls seconds behind me, bucking into me roughly until his thrusts steadily subside and he falls forward against me.

"Is it always going to feel this good?" he says, voice scratchy and exhausted.

I hope so.

Slice Sixteen

WINSTON

There are very few things I'm certain about in this life.

The St. Louis Blues are the greatest hockey team there ever was.

Slayer is the ultimate metal band.

I was born to wield a camera in my hands.

And I am steadily falling in love with Drew Woods.

It's not just the sex, though it's easily the best I've ever had. It's more than that.

It's the way she takes care of her son and everyone else around her...*before* herself. Her resilience. Her tenacity. The smartass comments. Her self-reliance.

Her really great rack.

Drew is the perfect package.

Last week when we had the house to ourselves and we fucked on the patio, I thought for sure I was going to spill my feelings all over the damn place like a fool when she asked me what we were doing.

Somehow, I reined them in and was able to shift the conversation more toward a topic she'd understand—sex.

I'm not ready to tell her, and she's not ready to hear it.

We're walking a careful line right now, and neither of us are ready to step over it.

"Are you ready yet?"

"Just a few more minutes…"

I look down at Riker, who is already strapped into his car seat. "Your mother is the slowest human on the planet."

"I can hear you, you know," Drew says from the bathroom where I guess she's still working on her makeup.

"Well, color me shocked, because I told you to be ready at five and it's now"—I check my cell phone—"five fifteen. We're gonna miss all the fun stuff."

"We are not. Quit being a baby. Just give me two more minutes."

Today is the first time we've had the same day off since the night on the back deck. I've upped my hours to full-time, trying to replenish my savings after paying for Drew's apartment and car. And, okay, maybe to prove to her I'm not a complete waste of space.

But my new full-time status is nothing compared to what Drew's been doing.

The crazy girl has been picking up at least three doubles a week on top of her full-time schedule because my father's finally letting her in the kitchen.

She's just on basic prep in the mornings and waiting tables in the afternoons, but prep is still the kitchen.

You'd think working so much and doing the mom thing in the evenings would be killing her, but it's done the opposite.

The only other time she's so alive and lit up is when I'm making her come, which I've been doing plenty often since we've been…well, whatever it is we're doing.

The bathroom door finally creaks open, and the moment she steps out, my dick springs to life.

On any given day, Drew Woods looks hot.

But tonight? She looks downright *edible.*

The bright red romper she's wearing makes her legs look a mile long. It makes me want to feel them around my waist again.

"See something you like, Winston?" she asks, lip between her teeth, round brown eyes peeking at me through her long, dark lashes.

"Fuck yeah I do. Come here."

She struts over to me, tucking herself between my spread legs.

I run my hands up the backs of her thighs, right under the short one-piece she's wearing, cupping her ass in my hands.

"You sure you don't want to just stay in tonight? I can think of a million things we could do that are going to be just as fun as the Fall Festival."

She giggles, her hands crashing into my hair, playing with the strands. "Weren't you the one just rushing me, all excited about going out?"

"Yes, but I wasn't aware you were going to come prancing out looking like *this.*"

"I don't prance."

"Oh, you prance." I squeeze her ass and she shuffles closer. "What do you say, Drew? Want me to peel this thing off you or what?"

"Good grief, you two. Do you ever stop screwing?"

Drew and I haven't exactly told anyone we're sleeping together because we don't know what any of this means other than it feels good, but since Sully lives here too, he kind of knows there's something up.

Or at least he's assumed that's what we're doing since he caught us kissing in the kitchen one day. He didn't say anything, just walked in, asked if he could get by to the sugar, grabbed a fresh cup of coffee, and walked back out.

That was it.

This is the first time he's mentioned it since.

"Do you ever stop wishing you were screwing?" I glance around Drew to Sully, who's standing at the doorway. "Seriously, man, you've lived with me for a while now and I've yet to see you bring a girl home. Isn't your hand tired?"

"Just because I don't bring anyone here doesn't mean I'm not getting any action."

I raise my brow at him. "Oh? Do tell."

"I thought you didn't like talking about your conquests," Drew says.

"Ah, but these aren't *my* conquests."

She lifts her eyes skyward. "You're hopeless."

"—ly devoted to you." I wink.

She groans, tossing her head back, trying to wrangle herself away from me. "On that note, I'm leaving."

"I am too," Sully says. "You guys have fun. I won't wait up."

"You sure you don't want to come with us?" Drew turns toward him, and I finally release her fully. "It's gonna be a good time."

"And watch you two make out all night? I see enough of that at home, but thanks."

"Your loss!" I call to him as he scurries down the hall toward his room.

"Is it just me or is he really chill about us…" She flicks her wrist between us. "Well, you know. This."

"I mean, we're grown-ass adults, Drew. What we do is our business and ours alone. Sully respects that."

"So you don't think he'll tell Wren, right?"

"No, definitely not."

"Good. I, uh, I'd just like to be the first one to tell her, you know? I don't want her finding out from Sully or Foster. She needs to hear it from me."

"I highly doubt she's going to care. If she does have anything to say, I'll just bring up the fact that she's sleeping with *my* best friend too. That'll shut down any issues she might have with it."

She grins. "Solid point." She bends toward Riker. "You ready to get to the festival, little man? We're gonna have so much fun. Pumpkin cookies, pumpkin cake, pumpkin pie, pumpkin coffee, pumpkin ice cream, pumpkin funnel cakes, pumpkin—"

"You sound like what's-his-nuts in *Forrest Gump*, only change out shrimp for pumpkin."

"You mean Bubba?"

"Sure. Whatever his name is. I have no clue. I hate that movie—it's boring as fuck. I could never sit through the entire thing."

"I'm sorry, I must be hearing things." She stands, grabbing Riker's car seat. "Did you just say you hate *Forrest Gump*?"

"Yep. Sure did."

"No wonder we can't seem to get along. You clearly have shit taste."

"We get along just fine in bed," I remind her.

"Ah, yes—our one redeeming factor."

"It's a pretty damn good saving grace, if I do say so myself." I take Riker from her. "Now let's get out of here before I show you just how good it can be."

I never bought into all the small-town-living hubbub. All the people in your business all the time and the same four festivals each year gets old real fast.

But the Fall Festival is my one exception.

I've gone every year since the inception, mostly because my mother had a huge hand in getting it started. She was a lover of all things autumn, but being in a summer beach town, everyone always looked right over arguably the best time of year.

And since spending time with Drew and Riker seems to be my new favorite pastime, I was pumped when I found out she had the night off and we could enjoy it together this year.

Now that I'm here, I'm annoyed because it's becoming clear to me that Drew has me pussy-whipped.

Every time she shoves a pumpkin whatever in my face and bats her eyes at me to try it, my mouth drops open.

If this shit didn't taste so damn good, I'd be aggravated that she has such power over me.

But in all honesty, I kind of like it. Being with her just feels so…easy.

Well, as easy as anything can be when it comes to us.

We argued about the radio station in the car on the way here. Then again when we were in line for tickets for food vouchers. Then again when Drew wanted to try the pumpkin pie *and* the pumpkin cake, wasting two vouchers on essentially the same thing.

Which is where we're at now, standing in line for pie *and* cake.

The booths are set up right next to each other.

I'm waiting for the cake with the stroller and Riker, and she's waiting for the pie, practically salivating over it.

"I'm telling you—the cake is going to be a thousand times more worth the ticket. You can buy a damn pumpkin pie at the grocery store any time you want. You can't get this cake all year long."

"But I want pie too, dammit," she whines, checking the line ahead of her for the millionth time.

"Wasn't it you telling me we can't always get what we want?"

"This is an entirely different situation. I can get exactly what I want. I have enough vouchers."

"You mean *we* have enough. We're supposed to be splitting those."

"I told you we should have bought more," she says.

"I didn't realize you were going to use them all for yourself for some basic-ass pie."

The people around us gape at me, the ones in the pie line shooting daggers.

"You're all fools," I mutter to them.

Drew shakes her head, trying to be angry, but I see her lips tic.

"Just wait. You're going to try this pie and it's going to change your life."

"You better shut your piehole," I warn.

"Nobody says that anymore unless they're like fifty."

"Riker, your mom is about to walk home, and that's going to suck for her, because it's a few miles and she has short legs."

"Riker, your mother is about to murder your best friend and stuff his body where nobody can find him."

"You just threatened me. I have witnesses!"

Everyone in line turns the other way, already pissed at me for hating on the pie.

"Traitors!" I yell.

Drew and I step up to the booths at the same time, order our respective desserts, and then meet off to the side.

We take a bite at the same time.

"Oh my god," she moans. "It's *so* good."

For the first time in my life, I'm jealous of food.

I want to be the only one to make her moan.

"Here, try it."

"Not in a million years," I sneer. I shovel another bite of heavenly pumpkin cake into my mouth. "Oh my god," I mimic. "It's *so* good."

"I bet it tastes like dirt."

"I bet it tastes better than your pussy."

She gasps. "Winston!"

"You're right. I take that back. Nothing tastes that good."

Her face turns beet red, and I feel real damn proud for making her blush.

She trowels another bite of pie into her mouth, trying not to look so embarrassed that my comment makes her flush.

We throw our plates away and continue through the festival, stopping at all the booths set up along the main strip of downtown because Drew *has* to talk to everyone.

"Why don't you set up a booth for your photography? I bet you could make a killing here."

"I don't know. These kinds of events aren't really my thing."

She slides her eyes my way. "You mean you're too afraid you're going to put too many expectations on yourself and end up hating the hobby you love so much."

I don't say anything, but we both know she's right.

"You know, for what it's worth, there are plenty of people out there who took their passion and made a career from it and are doing just fine. I mean, hell, your twin sister did just that and she's thriving. Her life has never been better. You could learn a lesson from her and take a chance once in a while."

"It's not that easy," I say.

"It's also not that complicated."

"Says the most complex person I know."

She shakes her head. "Whatever. Just keep living in that safe bubble of yours, not doing anything about your life because you're too big of a pussy. You—"

"Well, well. Fancy seeing you two here together."

Two familiar faces from Slice, an older married couple named Blythe and Randy, stroll up to us. They've been coming to the joint since the doors opened. They're kind of like extended family at this point.

Randy bends down toward Riker. "Sorry, little dude. I didn't see you there. I take back my two and add a plus one."

Riker grins like he can understand him.

I stick my hand out to the older gentleman. "Randy, Blythe. Good to see you both."

"What are you two over here arguing about?" Blythe inquires.

"Nothing, ma'am."

"Oh bullshit," Drew says. "I'm trying to convince Winston here to do something with the skill he was given and has spent years honing. He's too afraid to take a damn chance on it."

"Are you crazy, boy? Your pictures are brilliant!"

Her response surprises me, because I know for a fact I've never sat Blythe down and showed her my stuff.

"You've seen my work?"

She points to her head. "Your sister does my hair, son. What else do you think I stare at while she's working her magic and taming this beast?"

"Sorry, Blythe." I grin at her. "Sometimes I forget your natural hair color isn't rainbow."

She bounces her short curls. "I look damn good with this hair."

"The most stunning woman here, present company included."

"Hey!" Drew exclaims.

"You mind if we chat a moment?" Randy asks. "In private."

"Uh, sure," I say. I look to Drew, who shrugs, having no idea what's going on either. "Be right back."

We walk about five yards away before he starts talking.

"Listen, Blythe and I are coming up on our fiftieth wedding

anniversary, and I'd love to do something real special for her. She's always jabbering about not having enough photos of us together, so I'd love to surprise her with a photoshoot or something like that. What do you say? Want to take a stab at something for us?"

Wait…

"You want me to…photograph you and Blythe? Like…professionally?"

"That's what you do, right? Take photos?"

"Well, yes, technically."

"Then you can do it?" Randy asks.

"Again, technically, I could."

"I'm not understanding."

Could I take photos for Randy and Blythe? Yeah, I could do that no problem.

But I don't *do* photography, at least not for people I know.

And I definitely don't take photos of people.

The coastline is what calls to me, and it's my main go-to for photography. Other than in Wren's salon, there isn't a single photo of mine hanging on a wall out there.

She pinky promised she'd never tell a soul where she got them, but I guess she let the cat out of the bag to Blythe.

Can't blame her, though. The old lady should have a job as an interrogator. She seems to be able to get anyone to talk.

"If you're not up for it, it's fine. I just figured I'd ask you before I went to some other local chump."

"I'm flattered you asked, really, it's just…I don't really *do* photography. It's sort of a hobby-only kind of thing."

He nods but looks disappointed. "I get it. Well, thanks anyway, kid. If you happen to change your mind between now and then, well, you know where I eat dinner three nights a week."

He winks, clapping me on the back, and we make our way back

to the ladies.

"What were you two gabbing about?" Blythe asks.

"We were just minding our own business," Randy smarts.

She ignores his quip and looks to me. "Listen, son, quit being afraid to chase what you want and buck up. You did it here with Drew, finally asking her out after pining for her for so long. You can do it with your photography too."

"Oh, we're not—"

"I'll take your advice to heart, ma'am," I say, interrupting Drew.

She stares at me, lips pulled into a firm line.

Blythe's eyes dart back and forth between us, a sly smile on her lips like something's dawning on her.

"Interesting," she murmurs. "Kids these days."

"I tuned out when I saw that the cake line is finally dying down, but I agree with everything my wife just said," Randy tells us. "I'm sure we'll see you two lovebirds tomorrow."

He shakes my hand again and heads toward the cake after bopping Riker on the nose.

"Think about what I said," Blythe says, patting my cheek. She leans in close and whispers, "Don't give up on her." She tosses me a wink before straightening up herself. "See you kids later."

When they're out of earshot, Drew spins toward me.

"What the hell was that?"

"What was what?" I say innocently, pushing the stroller forward.

"You know what I mean," she says out of the corner of her mouth, clearly annoyed with me. "Why did you just let them believe we're dating?"

"Because it's not that big of a deal if they think it."

"But it's not true."

"Am I really that awful that anyone thinking we're dating upsets you? Even if it's two old farts like Randy and Blythe?"

She grins. "I am ninety-five percent certain Randy would kick your ass if he heard you calling him an old fart."

"He'd definitely give it his best shot, but that's not the point. I just don't understand how you can fuck me every night and sleep in the same bed as me and live under my roof but be too chickenshit to call this what it is."

"Call this what it is? What?" She wrinkles her nose. "A relationship?"

I laugh disdainfully at her disgust, which is an obvious coverup for how she really feels.

"You say I'm living in a bubble, too afraid to go after what I want, Drew? Maybe you're right, but I'm not the only one doing it."

"What? What does that even mean?"

"It means there is clearly something between us, and it's not just mind-blowing sex. I'm saying maybe, just fucking maybe, you don't hate me at all."

"I'm not the only one doing the hating around here. You don't like me just as much as I don't like you," she maintains.

"*Or*," I say, "maybe that's not the case at all."

"Wait a second…are you…are you saying you *like* me?"

Her mouth is popped open, like even she can't believe the words coming out of her mouth.

But she should, because they're accurate.

Hell, they're more than accurate.

I like Drew, and I might even love her.

I just wish she could see what's right in front of her.

"I'm just saying maybe things aren't what they appear to be."

"Stop."

"Stop what?"

"Stop playing with me right now. I don't know what this is, but it's not funny."

"I'm not playing any game," I push out through gritted teeth, already annoyed with myself for opening my trap because she's obviously not taking me seriously. "I'm simply telling you I don't think the idea of us being together is entirely insane."

"You can't be serious. We can't stand each other!"

"No, Drew, you can't stand me. You've *never* liked me."

"That's not true," she says.

"It's not?"

"No. Actually, the first time I met you, I thought you were…charming. A little obnoxious because, I mean, you *were* staring at my tits, but still charming in your own way."

"What changed?"

"Honestly? You did. After your accident, you were just so…cruel, and not just to me. That part I would have been fine with, but you were terrible to your dad and your sister and it just made me really fucking angry because they were trying so hard to be there for you and you wouldn't let them. You had people who loved you, who wanted to take care of you, yet you just shut them out like they didn't matter. You stopped showing up to work. I mean, not that you had a great track record for that before the accident, but it was way worse after. Then you just…I don't know, gave up." She scoffs. "And that *really* pissed me off because of what you had right there at your fingertips: love and support. You just didn't give a shit about any of it."

I don't say anything, because her points are valid.

I was just in so much pain for so long that it morphed into anger. I know it's my own fault in a way because I gave up, but to anyone looking in, they wouldn't get it, wouldn't understand how hard it was to get up every day and trying to live like I wasn't in agony.

Giving up was easier. Smoking myself numb was easier.

I wanted easy.

"I don't hate you, Winston. I'm just really fucking annoyed by you."

I laugh. "You annoy me too."

"See? That!" She points to me. "That right there. It's why we could never work. We annoy each other too much. One of us would commit murder within the first six months. I just know it. A prison romance doesn't sound appealing to me."

"*Or*—and hear me out here—we could, I don't know, actually make it work. Sure, we'd still fight, but just think of all the makeup sex we could have."

She slams her mouth closed. Opens it.

Her wheels are turning. I just can't tell if she's thinking about what I'm saying and taking my proposal seriously or trying to find a way to let me down easily.

I'm too scared to find out.

"Winston, I—"

"Let's not talk about it, okay? Let's just enjoy the rest of the night. We have more pumpkin shit to eat and I want to enjoy it without you gaping at me like I have two heads."

For a moment, she looks like she wants to argue.

But it never comes.

Her eyes flit to my cock.

"Well, you do technically have two heads."

My lips tug up at the corners. "Shut the hell up and come on."

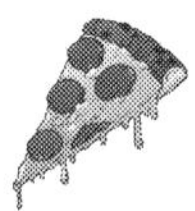

"Holy fuck," she mutters, coming down from her high.

I pull out of her, not wanting to leave her warmth but knowing I need to before I fall asleep on top of her.

"I think I just came so hard I pulled something in my back. It feels like I'm being stabbed."

I laugh, rolling away and flopping down onto the bed beside her. "I mean, you're welcome."

She reaches back to massage her injury.

"Wait, nope." She pulls something out from under her. "It was just a binky."

"I'm still taking credit."

"Not fair. It was literally a binky. You saw it."

"It's dark in here. You could have planted it after the fact."

She huffs. "Whatever. I'm going pee."

She rushes off to the bathroom and I let my eyes fall closed, trying hard not to fall asleep, but it's a difficult feat because I am officially worn out.

We didn't talk about us again the rest of the night, just enjoyed the Fall Festival.

Despite our bickering and Drew having a hard time seeing a future in us, it was still easily one of my top five nights of all time.

And that's not including the incredible sex we just had.

Being with her and Riker, getting to spend time with them doing silly shit…it fulfills me in a way I didn't realize I needed.

It makes me feel so…alive.

I could see myself doing it for good, not just while Drew's staying here.

The light in the bathroom clicks off and Drew tiptoes her way back to the bed, crawling in beside me with her cold feet.

She must think I'm asleep, because she doesn't say anything, just snuggles into me like she was made to fit beside me.

"Why can't it always be like this?" she whispers to herself, so quietly I almost wonder if it's all a dream.

If so, I don't ever want to wake up from it.

Slice Seventeen

DREW

The last few weeks have flown by, and I'm sad my time in the Slice kitchen is coming to an end after my shift today.

When Simon asked me to cover for one of the chefs who had taken a four-week internship in Italy, I jumped at the chance.

I knew the hours were going to be brutal, but the experience would be worth it.

All it has done is solidify my conviction that the kitchen is exactly where I am meant to be. It's my happy place.

"You're a damn natural in here, Drew." Simon stands next to me, watching me wield the knife in my hand like a pro, a proud glint in his eyes. "I wish I could keep you around."

"Then why don't you?" I beg him with my eyes to do just that.

"You know I can't, kid. I'd love to, but you need the training, the certifications. Everyone else here has them, and you need them too. It's the rules of my shop. And, really, it'll help you in the long run. You don't *have* to have any sort of professional training, but you'll be better off if you do."

"I know." I sigh. "I just have no idea how I'm going to swing that with working and taking care of Riker all on my own."

"It'll be tough, but I know you've got it in you. Besides, you already know you have a job waiting for you when you get out. That's the hardest battle."

"That's true."

"And then, when you get a couple years of experience under your belt working here, I'll write an incredible recommendation for wherever you choose to go."

"Leave you? Never."

"You better," he says. "I don't want you wasting your talents."

"But I love it here."

"I love it here too, but this isn't your end all, be all like it is mine. Slice is just a stepping stone for you, and that's perfectly okay."

"Do you really think I could make a career out of my culinary skills?"

"I guarantee that with a decade of true experience under your belt, you could start this town's first five-star restaurant and thrive."

I grin. "That sounds like an amazing dream."

"Then make it happen, kid. Only one who can do it is you." He winks at me. "Speaking of making things happen…I don't know what's going on with you and my son, but whatever you're doing, whatever motivation you're feeding him, keep it up."

"What do you mean?" I ask, peeking up at him.

"It's almost like we have the old Winston back, that guy he was before the accident—the one who was way less of a jerk." He looks at me. "Pro parenting tip: it's okay to call your kids jerks. Sometimes they need to hear it, especially from you."

"Noted." I laugh. "I'm really glad Winston's turning his shit around, but I don't think it has anything to do with me. I haven't even been pushing him to do anything extra. I've just been worrying about my own crap."

"I think that's it, though. I think he sees you struggling and not falling apart and it's giving him the kick in the ass he needs. Plus, I think he's trying to impress you."

My hands, which have been steadily chopping since Simon walked over, falter for the first time, and I pray he doesn't notice.

As much as I've tried not to think about the conversation Winston and I had at the Fall Festival on Sunday, it keeps pushing its way into my head.

Like now.

Simon isn't wrong. His son *is* different lately, and I'm starting to think I am the reason.

Winston Daniels, the man I hate, likes me…and not just in the bedroom.

When he dropped the bomb that he doesn't detest the idea of us being together, I was shocked, because I thought I was the only one whose mind that thought had crossed.

If I'm being completely honest with myself, I like Winston too.

But the thought of telling him and giving him the power to hurt me…it terrifies me.

Winston could either love me for a lifetime or shatter me in two.

There is no in-between when it comes to us, and that's one hell of a gamble to take.

"Impress me?" I scrunch my nose, trying to play it off like I have no idea what he means. Nobody other than Sully knows about Winston and me, and I'd like to keep it that way until I can figure out just exactly what's going on between us. "What for?"

He pins me with a *don't bullshit a bullshitter* look. "You know exactly what for. That boy has a heart-on for you."

"Ah, so *you're* where he got that term from."

"Actually, it was his mother. She used to say it all the time to freak the kids out because it sounded so much like hard-on."

I grimace.

"See?" He laughs. "That's the exact face they'd make."

"For a good reason."

"Anyway, I've been around long enough to know a heart-on when I see one. He might not be the world's greatest employee and he's a huge pain in my ass, but he loves harder than anyone else I've ever met." He looks at me meaningfully. "Just something to keep in mind if you're ever at a point where that's something to take into consideration."

"I'll, uh, keep it in mind," I say.

He grins, only it doesn't look natural. It looks too much like an *I'm onto you* kind of grin. Ominous.

If I didn't know any better, it almost sounds like Simon knows there's something going on between us.

But that can't be the case. We've been careful.

I mean, there was that one time Winston snuck a kiss on my cheek in the hallway and I ripped him a new one, but nobody saw us.

They couldn't have.

"If you need someone to help you look at culinary programs, I'd be happy to help."

I blink up at him. "Huh?"

"You know, for the certifications we were discussing," he explains. "Geez, kid, you lose your head that fast?"

"Sorry." I give myself a shake. "Brain is all jumbled."

"Right. Well, I don't want to distract you too much. We only have thirty minutes until open and there's still plenty to do. Just think about what I said."

What he said? Which part?

The one where he implied that he knows there's something happening with me and his son, or the one where he offered to help me create the future I want for myself?

Either way, they both feel earth-shattering.

It's evening by the time I drag my tired feet out the door of Slice. I am in no mood to make dinner when I get home, so I stop at Grab 'N' Grocery for something quick and satisfying.

The lights are turned down low when I finally push open the door of Winston's house.

"H-Hello?" I call out cautiously.

"In the kitchen," Winston answers back.

The weird just keeps on coming, because the kitchen isn't a place where he typically hangs out. In fact, I'm not so sure he even used it before I started living here.

I kick off my shoes, setting my purse down on the table by the door, and pad into the kitchen, bracing myself for something strange because it seems to be the turn this night has taken.

When I cross the threshold, I'm glued into place.

Winston's sitting at the dinner table, Riker beside him strapped into his boppy chair, looking like a mini adult sitting on his own as he's fed some disgusting-looking green mush.

From the looks of it, Riker isn't the only one getting fed.

The placemats, which I'm sure Winston had to rip the tags off of, are adorned with heaping plates of pasta.

It's nothing over the top. There are no candles or flowers or anything romantic.

It's simply dinner.

"What's all this?"

"Food."

"Yes, I can see that," I say, making my way to the refrigerator to stash my goods from the store. "But why? What's the occasion?"

"There isn't one. I knew today was your last day pulling doubles and I figured you wouldn't be too pumped to make dinner tonight, so I took charge and made something."

"You made something?"

"With my hands? No. But with my credit card and ordering capabilities? Yes."

Chuckling, I brush my hand over my son's head, bending to give him a quick kiss. "Mommy missed you today, little angel. I hope you were good."

I look to Winston for the answer, since he was the one who took over babysitting duties for the day.

"We had loads of fun. Lots of naps for some reason."

"It's the teething. It's wearing him out."

"It's wearing *me* out."

I wince. "I'm sorry about that. I'll be around to help out more now that I'm done with the doubles."

"No need to apologize. As weird as it is for me to say, I actually enjoy spending time with him. It's neat getting to see him learn new things every day. Kind of like this."

Winston shoots his brows up, and Riker, though he takes a few seconds to register it, mimics him.

I laugh and whip out my phone to capture the moment. I make Winston do it over and over, getting it on video and snapping a few pictures.

"When he wasn't napping, that was basically all we did today."

"I love it. I'm kind of sad I couldn't be here to watch him do it the first time."

"Don't do that, Drew."

"Do what?"

"Guilt yourself for having a life. You won't always be there for every moment and that's perfectly okay. When you're not there, I'll be there. Between the two of us, we'll capture it all."

His words sound so…permanent.

So…real.

So right.

Simon's words from earlier ring in my head.

He loves harder than anyone else I've ever met.

His words…his promise…sounded a whole lot like what someone in love would say.

Does Winston…*love me*?

I clear my throat, pushing the thought away, trying to not get my hopes up because the likelihood of Winston loving me is pretty damn slim.

"Thank you for dinner," I say, picking up my fork and digging in. "You read my mind on getting something easy. I actually stopped by Grab 'N' Grocery on my way home, figured we could just have frozen burritos or something. This is much better than my idea."

"We'll do burritos tomorrow then."

"Two days of laziness?" I mock gasp. "How bold."

"Bold or just ingenious?"

"Yes." I laugh, taking a bite of the pasta. "Holy crap. This is delicious."

"Wish I could take credit, but it's all my father's cooking."

"You were at Slice today?"

"Nah. I had it delivered. Figured it was easier than loading up the kiddo and taking him in. Plus, I knew if you saw him there, you'd get distracted and fawn all over him."

The kiddo.

Not *your* kiddo.

He says it like Riker is his too.

It's odd…but it doesn't feel wrong.

"Another smart move."

"What can I say? I'm on a roll today."

I scarf down my dinner like I haven't eaten all day, and I realize then I haven't had anything since breakfast.

"Damn, someone was hungry."

"I forgot to take a lunch."

"You forgot? How the hell does that happen?"

I shrug. "I was busy. Your father offered to help me look into local culinary programs and we spent my lunch break doing that."

"You're thinking of going to school?"

"I think so. I mean, I kind of have to, right? If I ever want to move on from Slice. As much as I love the pizzeria and get a kick out of whatever craziness your dad cooks up for a new pie, one day I'd like to be able to create my own menu." I peek over at him. "Do you think I'm crazy for wanting to go to school with everything else I have going on?"

"Crazy? Yeah, a little. I see how stressed you are as it is, but I also think it's a pretty brilliant idea to set yourself up for a future you really want. I know right now might seem like an insane time to do it, but it might be smart too, since you have the help."

"The help?"

"Living here."

"Winston…" I grumble. "We've been over this. I can't stay here forever."

"We've also been over that you *can*. You just don't want to hear that part." He pushes up from the table, grabbing his empty plate and mine. "But that's fine. You'll hear it when you're ready to."

"I'll listen to you when you listen to me about going to the doctor about your shoulder. How's that for a deal?"

He works his jaw back and forth, annoyed at my bargaining because he doesn't *want* to go back to the doctor.

He's too scared to hear that he and he alone screwed his shoulder up for good.

"That's what I thought," I say, grabbing Riker from his chair. "I'm going to give him a bath while you stew."

"I don't stew!" he hollers after me, but judging by the muttering, he knows he doesn't sound the least bit convincing to either of us.

I take my time bathing my son, enjoying my alone time with him.

When he starts to struggle to hold his tired eyes open, I click on the Slayer mobile and tuck him into his crib, grabbing the baby monitor on my way out.

Walking through the living room, I spy Winston out on the back deck, cigarette in hand.

I don't have to be standing next to him to know he's thinking about my comment. I can see it in the way his muscles are tightened, the way he's angrily flicking his ashes into the tray.

He's staring out at the water, letting the sounds of the waves drown out whatever's going on in his head.

Except it's not working, because deep down he knows I'm right.

I like Winston, and he clearly likes me.

But we can't push this thing between us another step forward until he addresses the thing that's holding him back.

Himself.

I force my feet to move, heading into the kitchen to grab the treat I bought to console myself after my last day in the kitchen.

Winston sends me a glance over his shoulder when I slide the back door open.

"Hey," I say quietly.

He grunts in response.

"Here." I slide a pint of ice cream toward him. "Thought you could use this."

He looks down at the offer then back at me. "Do I look like a basic white girl?"

"Excuse me? Pumpkin ice cream is the *best* ice cream."

He chortles. "It is pretty damn good." After popping the lid on the container, he holds out his hand. "Spoon me, woman."

"Spooning leads to forking, you know." I waggle my brows, handing him a utensil.

"Is that a promise of what's to come tonight?"

"Maybe." I smirk. "I wouldn't be opposed."

It's been four days since we last had sex, which is practically a dry spell for us.

I've just been so tired when I come home from work that I fall right into bed after taking care of Riker.

"I'm being serious, Drew—if you want to continue staying here while you go to culinary school, you're more than welcome to. It'll help cut down on expenses, allowing you to work less and focus more on school. Plus, between me and Sully, we can keep Riker out of daycare to cut costs there too."

My immediate thought is to say no, to refute his offer like I've already done.

But he's making many valid points.

It would save me money, yes, but would living with Winston save my sanity? Admittedly, these last few weeks have been better between us, but that could easily be attributed to me not being here all that often.

I don't want to bank my future on a few good weeks.

If I'm going to do this—go to school, work, and care for my son—I'll need stability.

I don't know if Winston's ready for that kind of commitment.

"You keep trying to convince me to stay forever and a girl might start thinking there's something more to your proposal."

"Maybe there is."

He sets his ice cream down on the railing then grabs mine from my hand and does the same. He pulls me toward him, his hands cupping my face and bringing it up to his.

"What?" I whisper when he doesn't say anything, just bores his eyes into mine.

"I've missed you."

"I've missed you too."

The words fall out of my mouth with ease, like missing Winston is the most natural thing in the world.

He runs his thumbs over my cheeks, his touch so gentle, so sweet.

The gentle strokes make my heart *thump thump thump* in my chest.

When he touches me softly like this, it feels like he's touching my soul.

"What are we doing, Winston?"

"I don't know anymore."

"What do you want to do?"

"I don't know that anymore either."

I swallow the lump forming in my throat. "I'm scared."

"Of what? Me?"

"Of us. We're just so…" I shake my head. "When we're good, we're explosive. When we're not…well, it sucks."

"Everyone has their ups and downs."

"But we have more downs than ups."

"That's not true," he argues, pulling my eyes back to his. "We've been doing great these last few weeks."

"Because I've been gone."

"Or because we're growing."

Maybe he's right. Maybe he's not.

Am I willing to take a huge chance and find out?

"All I know, Drew, is that I like you. I like spending time with you. I like spending time with your son, and I don't hate the idea of doing so for a long time."

"I don't hate that idea either," I admit. "Remember that first night we almost slept together?"

"You mean when you were too afraid to admit you wanted me?"

"Yes, that night. Do you remember what you said to me?"

"What about it?"

"If you aren't one hundred percent certain you want to do this with *me* and not just because it feels good to have *someone* here, walk away. We can go back to being friends like nothing ever happened. I'm really good at faking it until I make it." I place my hand over his heart, feeling it beat wildly beneath my palm. Mine's doing the same thing. "Because if we do this, Winston, if we say we're together and we take that next step, there's no turning back, no pretending this didn't happen. I'll get attached. Riker will get attached. You'll get attached, and if the bottom drops out from underneath us, we're both screwed. You have to be sure you're ready for this, because you're not just taking on me. It's my son too. This isn't playing house. This is for real. Are you ready for that? Are you ready for *us*?"

He opens his mouth, but I shake my head.

"No. Don't say anything right now. This can't be a hasty, in-the-moment decision. I need you to think about this, long and hard. Let it percolate for at least forty-eight hours before you give me an answer."

He nods. "Fine, I can do that. But, Drew?"

"Yeah?"

"You said long and hard."

I crack a smile. "I still hate you."

"I still hate you too."

Slice Eighteen

WINSTON

"Is it April Fool's Day or something?"

"No."

"Then what the hell are you doing here at this hour? You've been late to work plenty of times, but never early."

I grunt at my father's attempt to be funny. "Don't quit your day job, Pops. Comedy is not your strong suit."

"What are you talking about? I'm hilarious. My employees laugh at my jokes all the time. And besides, Beth thinks I'm a hoot. Right, hon?"

My dad's girlfriend smiles. "Right."

"Your employees laugh because they're afraid you'll fire them. Beth laughs because you're knocking boots." I wink at her. "Right, hon?"

Beth tries to hold in her laugh, because we both know I'm right.

"You"—he points to Beth—"are so on my shit list now."

"I'm shaking in my boots," she taunts.

"They the same ones you wear when we're knocking them?" He waggles his brows at her.

"Ugh, Dad." I gag. "Can you just not?"

He laughs. "Where's your sister? She's my new favorite. You're no fun."

"She's always your favorite, you mean," I say, taking a seat across from him in his office.

His brows lower and he frowns. "That's not true. I love you both equally…in general."

"In general? Oh, please elaborate. I'm dying to hear exactly what that means."

Beth squeaks and presses a kiss to his cheek. "I'll leave you two be. This sounds like it might get serious."

She gives me a wave and closes the door behind her, leaving my dad and me alone.

"I just mean your sister is a little more…pleasant to deal with on most days."

"So what you mean to say is I'm a dick?"

"Yes."

I sputter out a laugh. "Gee, thanks."

"Hey, that's no one's fault but your own."

"Drew thinks I'm a grump too."

"She isn't wrong," he agrees, shuffling some papers around. "How's that going, by the way? Her living there with her son and all, I mean."

I'm not stupid. I can read between his words.

He wants to know what's up between us.

"You already know I like her, so just ask me what you want to ask me and stop beating around the bush."

"Yes, we established that long ago when you showed up with bruised knuckles after you beat the shit out of that deadbeat ex of hers. You ever tell her about that?"

"I told her as much as she needs to know."

He nods, accepting my answer. He wasn't happy with me resorting to violence, but I don't think he was as opposed to it as he should have been either.

Drew is like a daughter to him, and he wanted to punch that dickbag Chadwick too.

"Are you freaking out having her there? Taking on raising a child is a big deal. Is that something you really want to do?"

"I think so."

"You think or you know so? Drew doesn't have a choice in raising her son. You do, so you better be real damn sure it's what you want. If it's not, pull back before you get too attached."

"Funny, she basically said the same thing to me last night. You two been talking?"

"No. She has no idea I know about you guys."

"Good, because I'm pretty sure she'd chop my balls off, and I'd rather that not be a thing. I'm kind of attached to them."

My dad snorts. "Literally. Anyway, I'm sure you didn't come in just to shoot the shit with your old man. What's up, son?"

My nerves start to get the better of me and I bounce my knee up and down as a distraction.

I've been thinking about what Drew said over twenty-four of the forty-eight hours, hours I don't actually need.

I already know I want to do this with her. I've *known* I want to. I've just been waiting on her to catch up.

Now that she's there, I know she's not going to just take my word for it, know I need to show her she can depend on me and I'm not the same grumpy bum she's always known me as. I need to show her I have drive, I'm reliable, and she can count on me.

I'm still scared shitless about taking the next step, worried I'll wake up one day hating the thing that brings me so much joy, but the thought of doing anything else scares me too.

So I guess I'll just have to take my chances and go for it.

The only way I'll find out if I'm going to fail is to try, right?

I blow out a steadying breath. "I was, uh, I was actually wondering if I could maybe do a shoot in the pizzeria."

"Like a photoshoot? What for?"

"For me."

"You want to take pictures of yourself in the pizzeria?" He leans across the desk. "Do you mean, like, a sexy photoshoot? Is this a weird kink you and Drew are into? Boudoir pizzeria shots?"

I bark out a laugh. "No. That is definitely *not* something we're into. At least I don't think we are."

"Oh." My father sits back. "Good. Because that'd be weird if your mom *and* you were into that."

"Dad!" I groan.

He shrugs. "What? Your mom was a wild card."

"Please. Just stop." I pinch the bridge of my nose. "I'm being serious here."

"I am too." He grins. "Okay, fine. What's this photoshoot idea you have?"

"Well, it's not actually *for* me. It's for my…well, my business."

His brows shoot up. "Your business?"

"Yes."

"For photography?"

"Yes."

"Oh."

He stares at me, and it's unsettling.

It's the same look Randy gave me when I pulled him aside earlier this week and told him I'd love to shoot him and Blythe.

Granted, his mind didn't go straight to photography, so he was really confused about why I was threatening him.

But that's beside the point.

I squirm uneasily in the usually comfortable chair, my dad's stare burning through me. "Are you going to say anything other than *oh*, or is that all you've got?"

"Sorry, I'm just surprised is all. You've always been so…shy about it."

"I have not."

"Yes, you have, which has always seemed silly to me because you're clearly extremely talented."

"You have to say crap like that—you're my dad."

"I am? Dammit, your mom never said I was Wren's dad *and* yours. That's bullshit."

"Your jokes are getting worse by the minute."

He smirks. "All right, fine. I guess what I'm saying is, I'm proud of you. It's about damn time, kid."

"Can we not make a big deal about this?"

"Hey, you're the one who walked in here being all serious and asking me permission like this isn't your restaurant too."

"But it's not."

"It's a *family* restaurant. You're my family. Therefore, it's *your* restaurant."

He's got me there.

"If I didn't know any better, I'd say you were actually coming here to get my approval."

"Pfft. I don't *need* your approval."

"No, but you want it."

He's right. "You're wrong."

"Uh-huh. Whatever you say, kid. But, in case I wasn't clear, the answer is yes. You are more than welcome to use the shop."

"Thanks, Pops. You're the best dad I've ever had."

"I'm your only dad."

"As far as you know." I push up out of the chair. "Well, I'm gonna get going. I have some stuff I gotta take care of before my shift. Oh, I almost forgot—I'll be late later."

"I am shocked," my dad deadpans. "Just shaken to my core."

I turn when I'm in the doorway. "Is Wren still your favorite now that I'm doing my photography thing for legit income?"

"No, you're definitely my favorite kid now."

"What the shit, Dad!" my sister yells, storming past me and into the room.

I leave them there to duke it out.

"So you're really doing this, huh?"

"I mean, I'm here, aren't I?" I lower my camera to scowl at my best friend, who has insisted on hovering around me during this entire shoot. "You're in my shot."

"I am not. I'm standing like a billion feet away from you."

"Your shadow is."

"Just Photoshop it out."

"Foster, I'm doing you a solid right now, and I will stab you. Move."

"Do you talk to all your clients this way?"

"You're not paying me," I remind him. "You're not my client right now. You're still just a friend. Murder is totally a viable option."

He nods. "That sounds fair."

I take a few more shots of the landscaping he's done to Wren's front lawn. It's nothing over the top, but it's clean and easy to take care of. People around here will eat this shit up. I've been following him around all week taking pictures of the few jobs he's done so he can add them to his website because my boy has his own business now.

Kids grow up so fast these days.

"So, what's up?" he asks, offering me a beer after I've finished shooting.

I wave him off, grabbing for a bottle of water since I have a shift at Slice I should be running off to. "What do you mean?"

"Why the sudden change of heart about shooting for cash?"

I raise a shoulder. "Just figured it's time."

"Right, and none of this has anything to do with a certain someone living with you now? She hasn't…inspired you to finally get off your ass and do something?"

"By 'inspired,' you do mean berated me over and over until I finally gave in?"

"Yes."

I glare at him. "She's not *not* inspiring me."

He laughs. "That's what I thought. I could kiss the girl for getting you to do what you should have been doing for years."

"Funny coming from you, the guy who bailed across the country to marry a girl he barely knew."

"Hey, dude, you know I had my reasons."

"Are you out here talking about kissing other girls?" Wren comes walking up the pathway to her house, eyes locked on us sitting on Foster's tailgate. "Because that's grounds for divorce, Foster."

"You can't divorce me when we're not even married yet."

"Only because you're *still* being a big baby about the wedding."

Foster sighs. "Drop it, Wren."

"Fine," she settles. "But at least tell me who you're out here talking about kissing. I need to know who my competition is and if I should be hitting the weights a little harder or not."

"Drew."

My sister's eyes flit to me, and a grin slowly pulls across her lips. "I knew it wouldn't take long for you two to start banging."

The sip of water I just took comes pouring out of me, dribbling down my chin in a wet mess. "What the fuck, Wren?"

"What? I'm just saying, your sexual tension has always been palpable. You two walk around pretending to hate each other all the time when all you really want to do is…" She humps the air. "Going at it like a bunch of damn bunnies, probably. And I'm glad. It was starting to get really old."

I shoot daggers at Foster. "Did you tell her?"

He holds his hands up in innocence. "I didn't say a peep."

"Wait a minute—you knew they were banging?"

"Well…" Foster grins. "I knew they were *finger*banging."

"Foster!" I growl.

"What? If you didn't want people to know, you shouldn't have snuck off during a damn baby shower to get down and dirty."

Wren gasps. "Oh my god. You two *banged* at the baby shower?"

"No."

"They were *finger*banging."

"Goddammit, Foster!" I shove him off the tailgate, and his laughing form crumples to the ground.

My shoulder pops—*loudly*.

Pain shoots up and down my arm, all the way to the tips of my fingers.

It's bad. Worse than it's ever been before.

Tears spring to my eyes and I try to blink them back, not wanting to cry in front of Foster and Wren.

Maybe they didn't even hear it.

"Was that what I think it was?"

Wren's eyes are on mine, and they're full of fire.

Okay, so maybe they did hear it.

"Dude, Winston, that can't be natural, man," Foster says, pushing himself up off the ground, staring at me with the pity I hate so much.

"It's not," I say, rubbing at my shoulder. "But I'm fine."

"You're not fine. *That* is not fine. Your eyes wouldn't be all bloodshot right now like you're trying not to cry if you were fine."

"Let it go, Wren."

"No, dammit! I won't." She stomps toward me, not stopping until her knees are touching mine. She has one hand on her hip, and the other is pointing a finger in my face. "You need help, Winston. You need to get back to your doctors because *that* is not okay. If you aren't going to do it for yourself, at least do it for the girl you're in love with."

My brows shoot up, and she rolls her eyes.

"I'm not stupid, Win. I've seen the way you've looked at her since she breezed into our lives. You've always had a thing for her. I just assumed it was because she has an amazing personality and is hot as fuck. I didn't realize your feelings were deeper until you moved her into your house. That was a dead giveaway because you don't let *anyone* into your house."

"Not true. I let Sully in."

"Because you saw something in him. You needed him at that point in your life, just like you need Drew."

"I don't *need* Drew."

"Maybe not, but you *want* her." Foster smirks. "You want her *bad*."

"Shut up," I grouse.

"Does she know?"

"Know what?"

"That you love her, you idiot." He rolls his eyes. "Have you told her?"

"Not explicitly, but I've put it out there that I want more."

"No, man. You gotta tell her. Just straight-up say it. That's what I did with Wren."

My twin nods. "It's true. He just came right out and told me what he wanted from the beginning. It was weird, being faced with something so forward, but it was easier. I knew what I was working with from the beginning."

"But we're not at the beginning. We've been doing…well, *this* for a while now."

"It."

"What?" I question Wren.

"You know…doing *it*." She humps the air again, bouncing her brows up and down. When I shake my head at her, she throws her hands up in the air. "What? It's true. It's not my fault my brother *and* my best friend are horndogs and can't keep their hands off each other."

Foster laughs at his fiancée, and I question why I keep these two around.

"Anyway, I digress," Wren says. "Just because you're not at the beginning doesn't mean you have to pussyfoot around what you want. Just tell her. I know Drew—she'll listen."

"Then you know she'll probably argue with me for about twenty minutes beforehand."

"But she will listen," she insists. "And she's worth the fight."

"She is," I agree, smiling at the thought of Drew standing before me, arms crossed over her chest. The angry version of her probably shouldn't turn me on so much, but it does. "Anyway, thanks for the pep talk, but I should probably be heading out. I have a short shift at Slice this afternoon."

"You do? Why?"

"Remember that bigshot football guy Dad hired?"

"Jonas Schwartz?"

I nod. "Yeah, him. Well, he was called away to the NFL or some crap like that, so Dad's short-staffed. I'll just be there covering a few gap hours."

"That's so…responsible of you." Wren smiles. "God, I love what being with Drew is doing to you."

I groan. "I make my own decisions, you know."

"Sure, but you also crave her approval, which is why you're being a good little worker bee like the rest of us. You want her to see you're responsible and reliable." Wren gasps, snapping her fingers. "Is that why you're starting your own photography business? To provide for her and Riker because you're gonna propose to Drew or something?"

My heart jumps into my throat.

"Slow your roll, turbo. We aren't even officially dating yet. Marriage isn't on the table."

"Not everyone is as insane as we are and gets engaged after less than a year of dating," Foster tells her.

"Yeah, but you've always had a pizza my heart. That's different."

"Did you really just say pizza?" I curl my lip, leaning away from her insanity. "That's it. I'm really leaving now." I hop off the bed of the truck and head toward my car. "See you guys later."

"Win, wait!"

I turn and Wren jogs toward me.

"Look, I know I've been razzing you about Drew, but I'm happy for you. I really am. I think you two work together. You push each other in the best kind of way. But, please, get your shoulder looked at. If not for yourself, for Drew." She gives me that same look Foster did—*pity*. "Please. I think something is seriously wrong."

"You think I don't know that? You think I haven't known that for the past few years? Why else do you think I've been smoking myself silly?"

She tilts her head, pursing her lips.

"To mask the pain, Wren."

"Oh. Huh. I just thought you were a super stoner or something."

I chuckle. "Nah. Well, I mean, yes, but also no. It was the only thing that helped me get through."

"Helped?"

"Yeah. I, uh, quit."

I don't know why I whisper it, like I'm ashamed or something.

There's nothing wrong with weed, nothing wrong with letting that buzz wash over you, but Drew was right when she called me on my shit.

I wasn't smoking because it's fun or because it was my only choice. I was doing it to take the easy way out, because I didn't want to work for my recovery, which is really unfair to myself and the people who *have* to use it to get by. I was making a mockery out of all of us.

Weed is a drug that is to be respected, and I was abusing the hell out of it.

"For Drew?" Wren asks.

I nod. "And me. I didn't like who it was making me."

Wren's eyes soften. "I'm sorry. I feel like I failed as your twin. I didn't realize you were hurting so bad, Win."

I shrug. "I didn't let anyone know. I shut down, shut everyone out."

"That part I did notice. You've been so…mean."

I wince. "I'm sorry. That wasn't me. It was the pot. I love you. You know that, right?"

She cringes at the mushy moment but says, "I love you too. But if you *really* loved me, you'd get your shoulder looked at."

"You and Drew really are best friends. She's been riding my ass about it too."

"See? That's two people who give a shit."

"Three!" Foster yells. "That's three!"

"Oh my god, quit eavesdropping before I come over there and beat your cheeks!"

"Did you just threaten to fuck him in front of me?"

"No. But also kind of yes." She rolls her eyes. "Anyway, *please*, Win, just do it. If Mom were here, she'd slap you right upside the head for being so stubborn and not taking care of yourself."

I grin, because she's right. My mom would totally beat my ass if she knew I wasn't doing what I need to do to be healthy.

"I'm starting to think this stubborn thing runs in the family, because you're stubborn too."

"I am not."

"You are too. You wouldn't even let me help you with your salon when I had the spare cash."

"Well, aren't you glad you didn't help me? Now you have more money for your shoulder." She winks. "Just do it."

"I'll look into it, okay?"

"You promise?"

"Yeah, sure."

"That's not a real promise, but it's probably the best I'll get out of you today, and I know better than to push my luck when it comes to you." She wraps her arms around me and squeezes me quickly. "Later, penis wrinkle."

"Later, twerp."

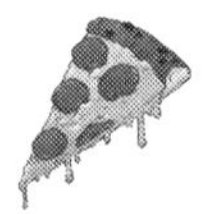

I could hardly contain myself all through my shift.

Drew was there for part of it, and every time she threw a glance my way, all I wanted to do was march over to her and tell her how I feel about her.

Lay it all on the line just like Foster said to do.

But since nobody is supposed to be privy to the details of us, I know she'd have my balls if I even tried to talk to her for more than a minute with everyone around.

So, I kept my distance, watched her from afar like a complete creeper.

I know she could tell something was up, because she kept sending me sharp glances, like she knew she was my prey and I was just waiting to strike.

I raced home as soon as I got off, not just so I could spend time with Riker, but so I could get everything in place, so when Drew comes home, I can say screw her stupid forty-eight-hour rule and tell her exactly how I feel about her.

But now that I'm in the thick of the nightly routine with Riker, all I want to do when she gets home is lay her down on our bed and show her how much I appreciate her because, fuck, all this baby crap is exhausting.

Feed. Bathe. Change.

Change again because he shit.

Put down for bed.

Feed again.

Change again.

I'm in awe of her.

"How do you expect me to get these penguin jammies on you when you won't stop wiggling?" I say to a freshly bathed Riker.

You can tell we've bonded because he didn't pee on me once during bath time *or* afterward when I was trying to get his diaper on.

We're making a lot of progress together.

He giggles at me, like he's taunting me or some shit, not helping one bit as I try to get his clothes over his constantly moving feet.

I frown at him, and he mimics me. "You're a little stinker. Anyone ever tell you that?"

He blows spit bubbles, laughing and tossing his legs about as I try to force the suit onto him. His legs might be little, but damn are they strong.

I hear my shoulder do that disgusting clicking thing it does and try not to wince at the pinch of pain.

I don't have time to focus on the hurt and feel sorry for myself.

Riker is my main priority right now.

It takes me another few minutes, but I finally manage to get his sleep jumper on and zipped. I'm nearly sweating by the time I'm done.

I stand him up on the end of the bed, his little hands wrapped around my fingers. He's smiling at me, looking pleased with himself for causing me to sweat.

"Damn, kid. Just got my workout in for the day with all that." He wiggles around, his little hands gripping my fingers tighter as he tries to hold himself steady. "Dang, Riker. Look at you go, standin' up. So strong, buddy."

More laughter and grins.

"Okay, you ready for some *SpongeBob* and bum time on the couch? Yeah? Come on, let's go be bums."

He wobbles forward, and I tighten my hold, only nothing happens in my shoulder.

It completely gives out.

And Riker goes tumbling headfirst off the bed.

Slice Nineteen

DREW

"Listen, Drew, don't freak out, okay? You have to promise not to freak out."

My heart plummets to the floor then flies back into my throat all within the same moment.

I try to take a deep breath, try to just breathe and keep calm.

"W-What's wrong?" I hear myself ask.

Maybe it's nothing. Maybe it has nothing to do with Riker.

I pace back and forth down the hall of Slice, worrying my lip between my teeth.

We're not technically allowed to have our phones on the floor, but Simon knows we all keep them on us anyway, and when mine started buzzing incessantly in my apron, I knew I had to answer.

"We're at the hospital."

We're at the hospital.

If I thought my heart sank before, I was wrong.

"Winston…what happened?"

"He's okay. He…he fell."

"How?"

"My shoulder."

My blood feels like it's on fire. His shoulder. *His fucking shoulder.* The same one he refused to get looked at. My son fell because of his stupidity.

"He's okay, though. We're just here as a precautionary measure. Sully brought us in. He—"

"I'm on my way."

Not able to stand another word from Winston, I end the call and shove my cell into my back pocket as I race down the hall toward the exit.

"Drew? Where are you—"

"Hospital!" I call to Simon over my shoulder as I charge out the front door of Slice.

"Hospital? What?" He tries to race after me, but I'm pulling open my car door and throwing it into reverse before he can even get outside.

I peel out of the lot, hook a right, and floor it to the hospital.

I don't bother to stop at the stop signs, blasting through them all.

Reckless, yes.

Necessary? Also yes.

I pull up to the hospital less than five minutes later, and it's one of the few times I'm so glad this town is as small as it is.

I don't even remember pulling into a parking spot, just sprinting through the emergency room doors, haggardly breathing as I approach the check-in station.

"Woods. Riker Woods."

"Relation?" asks the nurse manning the station.

"Do I look like a concerned neighbor? I'm his mother."

She nods, mouth pinched tightly. "Right this way, ma'am."

The woman leads me back into a cold, sterile hallway.

Behind a curtain, I can see Winston's feet as he paces back and forth.

I realize then I have to face him.

I don't want to face him.

The nurse pulls the curtain back. "I'll get your doctor for you."

I don't even bother looking at Winston, who knows better than to try to get in my way as I barge past him to my son.

Riker's lying in a crib, his eyes seeking me out. He grins the moment he recognizes me, and I choke back a sob at the sight of him, relief washing over me.

Minus the bruise forming on his head, he looks okay.

I reach into the crib, running my thumb over his chubby cheeks.

"Hey, angel. How you doing? You okay?" He coos, and I want to pick him up so badly. "I'm sorry, buddy. I am so, so sorry."

Winston comes to stand behind me, so close I can feel the heat radiating off him.

Glancing back at him, I let my eyes travel up his body.

He's wearing those boots I love and the jeans that hug his ass just right. There's a flannel shirt tied around his waist. If it wasn't for the sling around his arm, he'd look just like he did the night he told me I was going home with him, the night this all began.

Funny, because I'm certain this is the night it will all end.

"I—" he starts.

"No."

"Drew—"

"I said no, Winston."

I ignore his sorrowful stare and turn back to my son, giving him all my attention.

"Ah, Mrs. Woods. So sorry we have to meet in circumstances such as this, but I'm Doctor Farewell."

"That's a bit macabre," I murmur.

The doctor cracks a smile. "Your husband said the same thing."

My eyes fly to Winston, who's standing there looking guilty for lying to the doctor.

I had to, he mouths.

"I'm sure he's filled you in," the doctor says, "but Riker is doing just fine. Luckily the drop wasn't far, and he landed on carpet, or else we'd be looking at a completely different situation here. Mr. Woods was smart to bring him in as a precaution, but the bump is minor and he's responding well to all tests, so there's no need to be worried. I'd say you guys are good to go as soon as we get his exit paperwork filled out. Probably another thirty minutes and you're free."

I give him a small smile. "Thank you, Doctor. May I pick him up?"

"Oh, yes, of course. I'm sure he'd love some mommy snuggles right about now."

I lean into the crib, slowly easing Riker into my arms.

"Hey, angel." I kiss his little red cheeks, trying not to look at the bump on his forehead because I'm afraid if I stare too long, I'll break. "I'm so glad you're okay."

I squeeze him close to me, and he coos, snuggling into my chest.

A sob breaks from my chest, because I know how lucky I am to be holding him right now.

The doctor clears his throat and steps toward Winston, nodding to his injured shoulder. "Please, Mr. Woods, I implore you, get that thing looked at as soon as possible for not only your sake, but your son's. This could have ended a lot worse, and I'm sure you'd rather not risk it happening again."

Winston dips his head. "I will. Thank you, sir."

Dr. Farewell bids us good night and disappears as quickly as he came in, pulling the curtain closed behind him.

As soon as he's out of earshot, I turn to Winston.

"What in *the fuck* happened?" I seethe. "Where did he fall from? Did you *drop* him, Winston?"

"No!" His face crumples. "Well, kind of, but not on purpose. I was getting him into his jammies, and he was holding on to my fingers, showing off how well he could stand. He bobbed forward and my shoulder just gave out under his weight. He rolled off the bed before I could catch him."

I can just picture it, Riker rolling off, smacking into the floor.

My heart lurches at the scene in my mind, and I want to cry.

I want to cry for my child.

I want to cry because I wasn't there.

I want to cry because I am so incredibly angry at Winston for being so irresponsible and allowing something like this to happen.

"Drew, I am so, so s—"

"Don't," I warn, holding Riker tighter. "Don't you dare. You did this, Winston. You did this with your stupid pride, with your impatience, with your inability to grow the fuck up and just take responsibility. Because you were too goddamn childish to push through physical therapy after you were literally handed a second chance at life, now my son's lying in a hospital bed with a bump the size of Texas on his head. We wouldn't be here right now if you'd just done what you were supposed to do. This is *your* fault."

"You think I don't know that, Drew? I'm fucking sick over this."

"Good! You should be! I trusted you with him."

"It wasn't *me*. My body gave out."

"*Because* of you. Why couldn't you just listen to me? Why couldn't you just get yourself checked out? Why didn't you tell me your shoulder was *that* bad? I wouldn't have left you with Riker if I'd known."

"That! That right there is why—because then you wouldn't have trusted me to watch him. You'd have been freaking out the entire time, worried something would happen."

I dart my eyes toward Riker's bruised head cradled against my chest. "Clearly that would have been a valid concern."

"Drew, I know my body. If I'd have thought I couldn't handle him, I would have told you. I would have never put him in harm's way."

"Then what happened, Winston? How did your arm give out and you have no warning?"

"I don't know, okay? It just happened. It popped really bad earlier today with Foster, but it was doing fine until I was getting him dressed. It clicked again, but it wasn't anything major. I was fine, and then I wasn't. It happened in a split second. It's not like I planned to hurt him."

His eyes are burning red, pleading with me to forgive him.

"I know that, Winston. I know you didn't hurt him on purpose, but it doesn't change the fact that you *did* hurt him." I blink away the hot tears that are threatening to spill. "You know your body isn't supposed to make noises like that and yet you've done nothing about it, despite me asking you to go see someone. You—"

"Want to know what I find funny, Drew?" He laughs harshly, shaking his head. "You keep bringing up how *you've* asked me to go see someone, like that's supposed to matter to me in this big way, but you won't even make this thing between us official. How am I supposed to act like I mean something to you when you act like I mean nothing? Like we're just playing house and I'm cute, fun Uncle Jesse while you're

Bob fucking Saget with your shit all together."

"I—"

"Mr. and Mrs. Woods? Riker's ready to head home," a nurse interrupts, pulling the curtain back. "Though we don't believe there is anything to worry about, we recommend you keep a watch on the little guy throughout the night, checking on him every few hours, okay?"

I nod. "Understood."

"I'll meet you at the front desk whenever you're ready."

She walks away, leaving the curtain open.

I peek at Winston, who's staring at me with a brokenness in his eyes as I breeze past him and follow the nurse from the room.

He's hurting right now, and I'm hurting too.

But right now, I need to focus all my energy on my son.

We check out from the hospital and I buckle Riker into my car.

"What are you doing?" I ask when Winston tries to pop open the passenger door.

"Riding home with you."

"No, you're not."

His brows slam together. "Yes, I am."

"It's really cute that you think that, Winston, but it's not happening. I'd rather not be around you right now. Drive yourself."

I care about Winston, but the last thing I want to do is ride home with him. I'm too angry, too afraid I'll say something I can't take back later. I need time to cool off.

"I don't have my car, and even if I did, if you haven't noticed, my arm is in a sling. I can't drive."

"If you haven't noticed, I don't give two shits. Take the fucking bus."

I climb into my car, crank it, and drive away, leaving him standing there staring after me.

Sully springs from the couch when I push the front door open.

"How is he?"

"He's good," I say, setting the car seat down. "Sleeping."

"Good. That's good. I left as soon as Winston called you. I didn't want to crowd the room and figured it would be best if I left."

"Thank you for taking them in," I say.

"How, uh, how is he?"

He doesn't have to say his name, and I'm a little thankful he doesn't.

"I don't know," I answer honestly.

Sully nods, lips turned down. "Look, I know you're upset, and you have every reason to be. You probably don't want to hear it right now, but just know the first thing Winston did was tend to Riker. He didn't give a shit about his shoulder or the pain. He pushed through it and made sure your son was okay. There wasn't a second where he wasn't completely focused on him, so don't think he wasn't taking care of him, okay?"

"He let him roll off the bed, Sully."

"His shoulder gave out."

"Because he refused to acknowledge he was in bad shape. That is completely on him. He knew he was hurting. He should have said something before I left my son in his care."

"You're right. He should have, but he was just trying to help you, Drew. He knows how hard you work, how much you sacrifice for your son. It wasn't done out of malicious intent. He did it out of love."

Love.

The word sends my heart hammering and I try to push the thoughts of romance away.

I'm mad. I'm supposed to be mad. I can't be thinking about love right now, especially not with Winston.

"When they put Riker in the bed…I've never seen Winston break like that. He…" He shakes his head. "It was hard to watch. He wouldn't even leave to get his shoulder looked at. The doctors came to him. Winston loves Riker, Drew. He loves that baby so much. Just remember that, okay? Remember the love he has for you both."

I don't say anything.

I can't.

"I'm going to head out for the night, give you guys some space."

Another nod.

Before I realize what's happening, Sully wraps me in his arms, hugging me close.

"It's okay to be mad, Drew, but it's also okay to forgive him." He presses a kiss to the top of my head. "I'll see you tomorrow."

Then he's gone, leaving just me and Riker to ourselves.

Hours pass before Winston comes creeping into the house.

I don't know if he took the bus or walked. Either way, I'm glad for the few hours' reprieve we've been provided.

It's quiet enough that I hear the key in the front door, bracing myself to face him again.

I hear his shoes hit the floor and the loud sigh he lets out when he leans against the front door.

He taps his head against the wood twice before pushing away and ambling down the hall.

"Fuck," he mutters, running into the living room table. "Stupid fucking table."

The door to the back patio slides open, then closed.

He stays out there for half an hour, and I lie here, eyes slammed closed, trying to talk myself out of going to him.

Finally, the door is slid open again.

Now all I want is for him to stay away.

I smell him before I see him: the faint scent of cigarettes and regret.

They both make me feel sick.

Then, he's standing in the doorway, eyes locked on the crib in the corner.

The one he bought for Riker, *built* for him.

Slowly, he peels his gaze away, moving his eyes to mine. His mouth opens like he wants to say something, but he closes it, thinking better of it.

He walks into the room, closing the door behind him.

I watch as he struggles to strip from his clothes, wincing at the pain in his shoulder.

Exhausted and out of breath, he climbs into the bed, sliding under the blankets. He's close enough for me to feel his warmth, but not his touch.

I miss it already.

"I'm sorry, Drew."

"I know, Winston."

"I didn't mean to hurt him. I didn't mean for any of this to happen. I should have listened to you. I should have gotten my shoulder looked at sooner. I should have been the person you wanted me to be."

"You should be that person for *you*, not for me."

His tongue darts out to wet his lips. "I know."

We don't say anything for a while, just lie here, not looking away.

He reaches up, his hand slipping under my pillow. He pulls mine out, locking our fingers together.

"Listen, Drew, I—"

"I love you, Winston. Okay?"

His eyes are wide, full of surprise.

"I fucking love you, but I am so, *so* incredibly angry at you that I can't even look at you right now. I just want to go to sleep and forget this night ever happened. Do you understand that?"

He nods. "Okay, but—"

"What did I just say? I don't want to talk. Just sleep."

Another nod. "Fine."

I close my eyes, unable to keep staring at him if I don't want to break.

I love Winston, and a part of me thinks he could love me too.

But I don't know if that's enough anymore.

The light filters through the blinds of Winston's way-too-bright room.

Winston.

Just the thought of him makes my heart ache.

Though my anger has died down since I first got the phone call, I'm still upset.

I could hardly sleep last night between getting up to check on Riker and all the thoughts flying through my mind.

I know Winston didn't do it on purpose. His shoulder gave out. It's not like he threw him off the bed. It was an accident and could have happened at any time, not just when he was taking care of Riker.

It was just unfortunate timing, and thankfully Riker is okay.

Still, I'm so pissed at Winston for his pigheadedness. Sure, I'm known to be stubborn myself, but I'd never put my son in harm's way.

Winston did.

Knowingly.

I'm having a hard time letting that go.

I take a deep breath, knowing I have to face him at some point, and roll over.

The bed is empty.

I listen, straining to hear if he's in the house.

Silence.

I pull myself from the bed, padding out to the living room, looking out at the deck.

Vacant.

I go back to the bedroom, looking and searching for a note, anything that will tell me where he's gone, if he's coming back.

Nothing.

Winston is gone.

The overwhelming feeling that I need to leave rushes over me like a raging river.

I can't be here. I can't do this. Not now.

I reach under the bed for the bag I stuffed there and begin to fill it.

Slice Twenty

WINSTON

I gaze up at my house, one foot on the steps, heart hammering like mad.

I loathed leaving our bed—it hasn't been *my* bed for weeks—this morning, detested leaving Drew to wake up without me there, but I had something I needed to take care of.

Now that I'm back, I'm scared to face her, scared she's going to want to leave because of what happened.

And I really, really don't want her to leave.

I don't know if I'd survive it.

Pushing the front door open as quietly as I can, I don't bother stopping to toe off my shoes, wanting to get back to Drew before she makes a decision I don't want her to make.

My worst fear comes true as I watch her shovel things into a bag.

"What the fuck are you doing?"

I don't mean to yell it, but it comes out that way anyway.

She startles, hand flying to her chest in fright.

I reach for my own heart, making sure it's still in my chest, because right now I feel like it's being stuffed into those bags right along with her clothes.

"Holy…" She huffs and puffs heavily. "Christ, Winston, you scared the shit out of me."

"What are you doing?" I repeat. "Are you packing?"

"What? No, I'm just getting a beach bag ready. I wanted some time out on the sand to clear my head. Did you think I was leaving you?"

"I…" I blow out a relieved breath, running a hand through my hair. "Fuck. I don't know. I mean, after last night, I wouldn't blame you."

She side-eyes me. "Please. That's not my style. Unlike you, I don't run from my problems."

"I was gone."

"Yeah, I noticed. So what?" She shrugs, going back to tossing things into her bag. "You disappearing or giving up when shit gets rough is nothing new."

As much as I wish she were, she's not wrong.

"I'm a shitbag, okay? I get it. I'm trying to be better."

She doesn't say anything, just continues to throw things into the bag.

I gnash my teeth together, pinching the bridge of my nose. "Can you stop packing for a minute so we can talk?"

She sighs, wrapping the shirt she's holding around her hands and taking a seat on the end of the bed.

In the same spot Riker fell from last night.

The bile that seems to just live at the back of my throat now tries to work its way up, and this time I barely swallow it back down in time.

"Fine. I'll start." She sits up straight. "I don't know if I can do this anymore, Winston."

"I thought you weren't leaving me," I say.

"I'm not. I told you, I don't run."

"Then what are you saying, Drew?"

"I'm saying…" She licks her lips, exhaling sharply. "I'm saying I don't know if this…us…is a good idea."

"Why not? Because of last night?"

"Kind of. I just…" She abruptly pushes up from the bed, like she can't sit still. "Last night was awful—for me, for Riker—and I know it was an accident. Accidents happen, but, Winston…if you can't commit to our most basic instinct as humans to cover our own asses, how can I depend on you to commit to us? To take care of Riker with me? Because if we do this, if we give in to this thing between us, it's not just me anymore. It's not just sex. It's a real, honest commitment to a whole new life, and I'm not sure you're ready for it."

"I am."

"I don't know that I can believe you."

Her voice is calm.

I hate how it makes me feel, like I want to puke and scream at the same time.

She's not wrong. I've spent so much time over the last few years running and hiding from all my responsibilities. I haven't been committed to anything. Hell, even photography, the thing I find the most joy in, isn't something I can commit to fully.

I give up on everything too easily.

Life, living, moving forward—I just let myself stall and stall and never actually go anywhere.

I can't keep giving up.

I can't keep living like I have been, so angry and closed off. I have to take charge of my life and do something, not just coast.

"You can. I've been doing things, settings things up."

She crosses her arms over her chest in the way that drives me crazy. "What does that even mean, Winston?"

"Photoshoots."

"What?" Her eyes flash with surprise.

"I've been doing photoshoots, working on a client list, building a legitimate portfolio. I'm turning my photography into a business."

"But you don't want to do that…"

"That's not entirely true. I've always wanted to. I just never had the gumption to do it. Now I do. It's what I *should* be doing. I'm doing it because it'll create something stable for our future. I'm doing it for you."

"No, Winston." She shakes her head. "I told you, I don't want you doing things for me. I want you doing them for *you*."

"I am. I'm doing it because I love you, and loving you…it makes me feel whole. I want to keeping feeling whole."

Her arms drop slowly, and she stands there, mouth falling open and closed.

She gulps.

"You…love me?"

I cross the room to her, unable to stay away for another second.

She lets me wrap my good arm around her, pulling her tightly against me as I can with the limited movement I have. There's no hesitation as she clings to me like we've been apart for years and not hours.

"Of course I love you. I *have* loved you, for a long damn time now, probably since I forced you to come home with me. Actually, no," I say, leaning back to look at her. "It was probably before that, way back when I asked you to deflower me and you just laughed in my face."

She chuckles softly. "You like it when I'm mean to you."

I shake my head, cupping her face with my hand. "No. I like it when you're *real* to me. You're the only one who doesn't let me just sit around and waste away. You push me."

"I annoy you."

"Well, yeah, but I let you get away with that because of the sex." I smirk, running my thumb along her pouty bottom lip. "In all seriousness, Drew, I'm glad you annoy me. It means whatever you're saying to me is the thing I need to hear the most. I don't want to drift along and never amount to anything. I've never wanted that. I've just always been too fucking scared to do anything until you came along and gave me a reason."

"You need to do this for you, though, Winston, not me," she maintains, eyes hard.

"You're missing the point—I *can't* do this on my own. Some people need to chase the gold stars in life, and you're mine."

"You don't need me as incentive. You *can* do this. You just choose not to."

"Fine then, whatever. It's however you want to spin it. The end is still the same, Drew."

"It is?"

I nod. "I choose this."

I drop my mouth to hers, capturing her sigh between my lips.

I pull away.

"I choose *you*."

Kiss.

"I choose Riker."

Another kiss.

"I choose a future."

Kiss.

"I choose *us*."

This time, I don't stop kissing her.

It's soft and chaste and full of promises I intend to keep.

I pull away eventually. "I want this, Drew. Okay? I'm not just saying that to pacify you. I want us. I know it's not going to be easy. I'm going to have to work relentlessly at it. I'm going to have to push my fears aside often, wade through everything with cautious feet, but you're worth it. Riker is worth it. *We're* worth it."

"Winston…" Her voice is breathless, and she squeezes her eyes shut for a moment. "I…I'm scared. What happens if you stall out again? What happens if you stop choosing this? If you stop choosing me?"

"I'll never stop choosing you, but just in case I do, you'll be there to annoy me back to life."

One corner of her mouth tilts up. "You *have* to get your shoulder checked out. You *have* to take care of yourself. It's nonnegotiable."

"It's already done."

"What?"

"That's where I was this morning—the doctor. I made the appointment last night. After I explained the gravity of my situation, how my girl was probably going to leave me if I didn't get my shit together, he took pity and fit me in immediately."

"What did he say?"

"That I'm an idiot."

She laughs. "We already knew that. What else did he say?"

"I screwed myself. I'll likely need another surgery to repair everything."

Her eyes drop shut. "I'm sorry, Winston."

"It's my own fault."

"I know, but it still sucks."

"It does." I place another quick kiss to her lips because I just can't help myself. "Look, Drew, I don't want you to think this is some speech to get you to forgive me for last night, and I *really* don't want you to think this is something I'm deciding *because of* last night. I wanted to tell you forty-eight hours ago that I love you, but I wanted *you* to be ready to hear it. I want this, all of this, with you."

"I want it too. It doesn't mean we don't have shit to work on, though. I'm still upset with you. I still want to strangle you half the time."

"I would expect nothing less."

She rests her head against my chest, smiling. I hold her tight.

"I still hate you, Winston, just so we're clear."

"I know, Drew. I still hate you too."

A Slice of the Future

WINSTON

"Come on, Daniels, just one more. You got this."

I raise the bar over my head with less effort than I've had to use in years. I love the way my muscles stretch, because for the first time in a long damn time, it's not a bad stretch.

My doctor was right. I screwed my shoulder enough to require another surgery to repair my obliterated rotator cuff, all because I was a whiny asshole who didn't want to follow through with my original plan for recovery.

If I could go back and slap past me, I would.

But, live and learn…and go thousands of dollars into debt, I guess.

I try not to think about it, though, pushing for a bonus rep.

"Showoff." My physical therapist, Carlos, grabs the bar, helping me set it on the rack. "Proud of ya, buddy. That was your last set. You are officially done with PT."

A sense of relief washes over me. Even though I'm fully aware I'm not done healing yet, I'm already on a better track than I was, and that's enough for me.

"Thanks." I shake his hand. "Really appreciate everything you've done, man. Thanks for not letting me give up."

"It was dicey there for a minute, but I'm glad we made it to the end."

I almost quit again.

I was at the same point I was at after my first surgery and everything felt like such bullshit. I wasn't getting better. I was stuck.

Or at least that was what it felt like.

Luckily, this time around I had a therapist—and of course Drew—who wouldn't let me bitch out, and I'm grateful for him.

"Me too. No offense, though, Carlos—I really hope I never see you again."

He laughs. "Feeling's mutual."

We shake hands again and I hit the front desk, checking out for the last time.

I walk back to my station wagon—she's still running like the magnificent beast she is—with a smile on my face, feeling like I'm on top of the world.

I check the time on my dashboard and—

"Fuck! I'm gonna be late."

Throwing the car into reverse, I hightail it out of the parking lot toward home.

I have just thirty minutes to get across town, shower, and get all three of us out the door on time.

My PT days are always intense, and I should have paid more attention to the time. I have a strict schedule I'm on and knew better than to linger at the front desk chatting with Susan.

Drew's depending on me to be there for her. I haven't let her down in the last five or so months we've been together, and I don't plan to start now.

Things between us haven't been magically easy, especially throwing my surgery and recovery into the mix, but we've been putting in the effort to make it work.

She enrolled in culinary school, leaving her less time to work at Slice, which means I had to step up and really get my photography business off the ground.

At first, she was against me starting the business. It wasn't because she didn't believe in me, because she always has, but because she thought I wasn't doing it out of sincere desire. I finally sat her down and showed her the thousands of photos I've taken over the years and even laid out the business model I've had saved since before my accident but never took the initiative on.

She understood then that the only thing that was holding me back was my own fear and basically told me how dumb I was for not believing in myself.

She's lucky her candor is a total turn-on.

With how hard I've been hitting the grind—and through Drew's constant encouragement—I'm already looking to turn a profit with Daniels' Digitals in the first year.

It's weird how sometimes what we fear the most ends up bringing us the most joy.

I can't believe there was ever a day when I was scared to take my love of photography to the next level.

I'm good at what I do. I know that—I've *known* that, but I never thought I was good-enough-to-have-a-waitlist kind of good.

These last few months have proven me wrong.

I pull into my driveway and take the stairs two at a time.

"Hey, I'm here!" I say, throwing open the front door.

Drew's standing with her arms crossed, glaring at me. "Were you flirting with Susan again?"

"What can I say?" I grin, crossing the room and sweeping her into my arms. "She's hot for an old broad."

I capture her lips in a kiss.

It'll never get old, coming home to her.

Sure, we'd been living together for a while before officially calling this what it is, but it didn't feel *just right* until we stopped being afraid and took that next step.

Now, it feels like Drew was always supposed to be here with me, like us being together was the plan all along.

Drew begins to melt into me but catches herself at the last minute, pushing away.

"Winston, we *cannot* be late."

"Then stop assaulting me so I can go shower."

"*You* kissed *me*!"

"Then stop being so damn kissable."

She shoves me toward the bedroom. "Go. We have to leave in less than ten minutes!"

"All right, all right. I'm going." I pull my shirt over my head in the middle of the living room. "But just so you know, this"—I wave my hand over my body, making my pecs jump—"is what you're missing out on."

She rolls her eyes. "Yes, the lint stuck to your belly button hairs is getting me so wet right now. Moister than a damn oyster."

I glance down. "Well, fuck."

"Go shower. And for god's sake, clean your damn belly button."

She shakes her head, heading down the hall to finish getting Riker ready, muttering the whole time about how she can't believe she's actually dating me.

I beeline to the shower, jumping in and out in under five minutes.

I'm tying my shoes just as Drew walks down the hall, ready to go.

"Oh, good. You're ready. Here, take this." She hands me the diaper bag then the baby. "I have to go grab my hat real quick."

She disappears through the kitchen, presumably heading for the laundry room.

I look down at Riker, who is already fighting sleep.

"I know, little man. Mommy wears me out too."

He grins.

"I heard that," she says, coming back through the living room, checking her phone. "One minute to spare. Let's do this."

We buckle into the car and head toward the culinary institute Drew's been attending.

Tonight, the students are hosting a special dinner for family and friends to celebrate the end of their first term. A three-course menu has been crafted and the entire night is treated like we're sitting down at a high-end restaurant.

We pull into the school with just five minutes to spare.

"I'm heading in," Drew says. "Wish me luck!"

She gives me a quick peck then presses a kiss to Riker's head and races off for the pre-dinner meeting.

I still have another half hour until I need to be in my seat, so I take my time getting inside.

"Damn." Wren whistles. "You clean up nice."

I hike Riker up on my waist as we approach Drew's cheering section, which has gathered outside the doors. "I know."

"I was talking to my nephew," she says, reaching for the baby.

"Oh my god. I can't believe we had to wear a suit and tie for this shit." Foster grabs at his collar. "I'm dying right now."

"Quit being a baby. You look hot. I'd beat your cheeks."

My dad groans. "Wren, please. I'd like to keep my appetite for the night."

"Oh, please," Beth says, "you're just as bad as they are half the time with the things you say."

"When can we go in?" Sully asks. "I'm starving."

"I think we're okay to go in now, but dinner doesn't start for a bit."

"I hope they have bread," he says, pulling open the doors.

Soft music drifts through the speakers set up by a stage. They're handing out a few awards before things get going, and I've got my fingers crossed Drew wins one.

We find our table and take our seats.

"Best seats in the house," Foster says. "I hope that means we get food first."

"Did none of you eat today or something?" Dad comments.

"I did," my best friend says. "But I've been busting my ass out in the heat all day. I'm fucking ravenous."

"I've had Drew's cooking before," Sully comments. "No way I'm ruining my appetite and filling up on junk. I wanna enjoy this."

"Hey, you moved out on your own. You could have easily been enjoying her cooking all along."

Sully moved out a month after Drew and I made things official. We tried talking him out of it, but he waved us off and packed his things.

As nice as it is having my room back and Riker in his own space, I kind of miss the hippie.

"You don't know what you have until it's gone," he sulks, picking at the breadbasket in the middle of the table.

"Ladies and gentlemen," Drew's instructor says into the microphone. "Our evening will begin shortly. If you could please take this time to use the restroom and turn off your cell phones, we'd appreciate your full attention for tonight's event."

There's a rustle around the room, chairs scraping back and people rushing off to the bathrooms.

I grab Riker out of his high chair. "I'll be right back. Gotta get this kiddo a fresh diaper real quick."

"I can take him," Wren offers.

"You sure?"

She points to a growing belly. "I could use the practice."

She scoops Riker away from me and grabs his diaper bag before disappearing.

I take my seat.

"Man, it's still so weird to see you acting all dad-like," Foster comments.

"It's weird knowing you're going to be a dad."

He gives me a dopey grin. "Isn't it?"

"It's weird *I'm* going to be a grandpa," my dad comments.

"Not really," I say. "You're already as old as one. It just kind of makes sense."

Beth nearly spits out her water at the comment and my dad glares at her as she laughs.

"What?" She smiles. "He's not wrong."

"You are so close to walking home tonight." He shakes his head at her, and she just lifts her shoulder, unafraid.

"Don't worry, Beth." Sully winks. "I'll give ya a ride home."

"Hey, watch it," my dad says, eying my old roommate warily. "I might be old, but I can still fight like a spring chicken."

"Yeah, watch out, Sully—Dad might break out his cane and whip your ass with it." Wren slides back into her chair with Riker. "I'm pretty sure Riker could take you, Dad."

"Only because I'd let him," he says. "Here, let me hold him. I haven't seen him all day."

"No way! It's my turn."

"Actually, it's *my* turn." I steal Riker back.

My dad laughs. "Just wait, Wren. Pretty soon you're going to be begging people to hold your baby for you."

It's true. She has no idea the long nights she's in for. I didn't come into Riker's life until he was three months old so I missed a lot of the really long ones, but these last few months of teething and growing have been hell with everything else Drew and I are pushing through.

Wren and Foster are in for some fun.

There's a tapping on the microphone, and we all turn our attention to the stage.

"Thank you so much for being here with us tonight. Let's all give a round of applause for our culinary students."

We stand and clap as Drew's class files onto the stage.

She blushes as we whistle and hoot, making much more noise than anyone else in the building.

I wave Riker's hand toward her, and Drew's smile widens.

"I know you're all probably starving," the instructor says as we take our seats again.

"Famished," Sully mutters.

"So we'll try to make the awards ceremony quick."

He flies through about five awards, and with each one, I see the hope in Drew's eyes dim.

She's been working so hard these past few months. She doesn't need an award to prove this is where she belongs, but I know she wants one.

I want one for her too.

"For our next award, we have the Ultimate Sacrifice Award. This award is given to the student who not only exemplifies excellence in the kitchen, always looking out for not just themselves but the other chefs and upholding the integrity of the kitchen, but who also pushes themselves outside of kitchen hours."

The instructor looks down the line of students.

"Drew Eunice Woods, can you please step forward?"

"Eunice?" Wren shouts. "No forking way! I would have never guessed that!"

My twin falls into a fit of laughter and Drew shoots daggers at her, trying her hardest not to laugh and be embarrassed all at once.

"Damn," Foster says. "I had ten bucks on Amanda. I thought for sure she was screwing with us."

"I had twenty on something really generic like Anne or Lynn," Sully broods, pulling his wallet out.

"Pay up," my dad says, giddy as hell. "Beth guessed it right all along."

"You guys *bet* on what her middle name is? You too, Beth?"

"You hustled us?" Wren's mouth drops open. "Damn, Dad, your girl has some big balls."

Beth shrugs. "I knew it from her application. Easy way to make some cash."

The instructor clears his throat and we all realize the entire room is staring at us.

"I just want to make it clear I know none of these people," my dad tells the crowd. "I'm with them."

He points to a random table, the occupants looking amongst one another, trying to figure out who invited him.

We all bust out laughing.

When we've finally settled down, Drew looks like she could murder us but also like she wants to hug us.

"Right then," the instructor continues, trying not to appear amused by our antics. "Drew, your fellow classmates nominated you for this award. Your dedication and strength in the kitchen are admirable, but more than that, your perseverance when you're not here is something we can all aspire to. We know you have a little one at home and your boyfriend recently underwent surgery, and clearly you have a fairly exhausting group of friends to deal with."

"Tell me about it," Drew says.

"But no matter the hardships, you haven't missed a single class and still go out of your way to help your fellow chefs. We just wanted to let you know we see you and appreciate you. We think you'll run a very tight kitchen one day, and we're honored to have you."

We break into applause when she's handed the award, and I've never been more proud of her than I am in this moment.

"That concludes the awards for the evening. Chefs, you have a five-minute break before you're to report to the kitchen."

The students disperse off the stage, and Drew heads right for us, looking annoyed and elated and amused all at once.

"I can't believe I invited you people."

"And by 'you people' you mean your favorite humans in the world, right?" Wren wraps her arms around Drew. "Congrats, Eunice."

She groans, hugging her back. "Shut up."

"Proud of you," Foster says, giving her a quick hug.

"Yeah, great job." Sully puts an arm around her. "But listen, can you bring my food out first?"

"Go eat some bread, Sullivan," my dad says, stealing Drew away and squeezing her tight. "I'm very proud of you, kiddo."

"Thanks, Simon. I wouldn't be here without you."

"You'd have gotten here eventually. I just gave ya a push." He winks at her. "Eunice."

She rolls her eyes, and they land on me.

I smile at her.

"Dude, Riker," I say, bending to him but not breaking eye contact with Drew. "Your mom is officially an award-winning chef. How lucky are we, huh?"

She walks over to us, pinching her son's cheeks. "Super lucky, because your skills in the kitchen are severely lacking."

"Hey, I can order a mean pizza."

"It doesn't count when I have to make it."

"You don't make it yet—you're still on prep," my dad interjects.

With Drew now in culinary school, my dad finally let up and allowed her in the kitchen. Even though she's not cooking yet, she's delighted to be in a real-life kitchen, and it's worth all the crazy hours she has to keep.

"I'm proud of you," I say quietly, wrapping one arm around her, Riker between us, my lips brushing against her ear.

"Thank you. I couldn't have done this without you."

"Somehow, Drew, I doubt that."

"No, I'm being serious, Winston. I couldn't have. If these last few months have taught me anything, it's that I want you. Not just this, but *you*. I *need* you."

My heart rate picks up and I swallow the lump that's formed in my throat.

"Say that again."

She grins. "I need you."

I sigh, resting my forehead against hers. "I still hate you, Drew."

"Well that's too bad, Winston, because I love you."

THE END

ACKNOWLEDGEMENTS

I have to give a massive thank you to my husband. These last few months of our lives have been insane, *and* I've been on deadline on top of all the other crazy. But your support never wavered. You stood by me and worked hard to take care of things so I could have *my* time. You have no idea what your sacrifices mean to me. Thank you for loving me through my crazy.

Once again, Samantha Weaver, you've knocked it out of the park with this cover. It's SO cute. Plus, Courtney and Jordan make the perfect Drew and Winston.

Mom, thanks for allowing us stay at your house and then let me abandon you to write. You're the best.

Laurie, I legit don't know what I'd do without you. YOU are the reason this book happened. You kept me on track and kept me motivated. Thank you.

To my team behind the scenes… Caitlin, Julie, Judy, Dani, and Allie, and Aimee. Thanks for helping make this book the best we could!

Teagan's Tidbits… I can't leave you all out. You're the cheese to my toasted bread. The peanut butter (that's applied to BOTH slices of bread) to my jelly. And the ranch to my pizza. Thank you for everything.

With love and unwavering gratitude,
Teagan

Other Titles by Teagan Hunter:

A Pizza My Heart

I Knead You Tonight

Let's Get Textual

I Wanna Text You Up

Can't Text This

Text Me Baby One More Time

We Are the Stars

If You Say So

Here's to Tomorrow

Here's to Yesterday

Here's to Forever: A Novella

Here's to Now

Want to be part of a fun reader group, gain access to exclusive content and giveaways, and get to know me a little more?

Join Teagan's Tidbits on Facebook!

Want to stay on top of my new releases?

Sign up for New Release Alerts!

TEAGAN HUNTER is a Missouri-raised gal, but currently lives in North Carolina with her US Marine husband, where she spends her days begging him for a cat. She survives off coffee, pizza, and sarcasm. When she's not writing, you can find her binge-watching various TV shows, especially Supernatural and *One Tree Hill*. She enjoys cold weather, buys more paperbacks than she'll ever read, and never says no to brownies.

You can find Teagan on Facebook:
https://www.facebook.com/teaganhunterwrites

Instagram:
https://www.instagram.com/teaganhunterwrites

Twitter:
https://twitter.com/THunterWrites

Her website:
http://teaganhunterwrites.com

Or contact her via email:
teaganhunterwrites@gmail.com

Made in the USA
Columbia, SC
27 November 2019

83977538R10152